The Book
of Affects

SUNDIAL HOUSE

The Book
of Affects

Marília Arnaud

Translated by

Ilze Duarte

SUNDIAL HOUSE

**SUNDIAL
HOUSE**

Book and cover design: Lisa Hamm

Proofreading: Lizdanelly López Chiclana

ISBN: 979-8-9879264-6-8

Contents

To my beloved father, Dirceu Arnaud,
and my wise friend, Ascendino Leite

[. . .] the essence of man is desire, an awareness of what in the body is called appetite. Thus, to say we are bodily appetite and physical desire is to say that the afflictions of the body are images that manifest in the soul as affective ideas or feelings. It is the relationship between the soul and the body and between them and the world that we term affective relationship.

—Marilena Chauí, Brazilian philosopher
Translated by Ilze Duarte

The Book
of Affects

Flesh and Agony

LOOK AT me, Eugênio, and listen. It has been a long time since we had a proper conversation. Maybe our real conversations only happened during those first years, when we would stay up all night talking about ourselves, our ambitions and projects, our friends. Remember how we would go from our bed to the kitchen table, from there to the balcony for one last cigarette, then back to our bed, and lie there sleepless, energized, full of hope? Indeed there was such a time, which I recall with the nostalgia inherent in things that will never be again, when your caressing gaze would soothe my heart, when you would tell me what I needed to hear, that our desire to be together was greater than ourselves, that we were enough in our dreams and truths. There was a time, Eugênio, when the light of your love was so intense it would blind me, and then all I had to do was keep my eyes closed and let myself be guided.

Don't worry. Nothing that I say today will make you suffer any more than you already have. I wish I were noble and generous like you, my dear. If that were the case, do you think we would have been spared these wounds? I don't know. I know so little about barely anything. What do we know, anyway, about ourselves and those we love? What is the truth we each hold? There is no doubt you know the texture of my skin, the traces of sleep in my mouth, the imperfections of my body, my mood swings and idiosyncrasies. You know when to keep your distance. You know the best time to talk to me, how to touch me, irritate me, and then calm me down. You think you know me well, Eugênio? Then explain to me why some years ago an unrelenting feeling of dissatisfaction came over me, and everywhere the ground would shift under my feet, while I would spin around upon myself, knocking over everything around me, everything crumbling down with me, my own existence becoming a menace. Can you picture a bird so accustomed to the comfort of its cage it has forgotten it has wings and then briefly catches sight of another bird and is reminded of its winged nature, and in recognition of its own body, ruffles its feathers as it tries to take flight only to find no space and return to its stillness, which only then reveals itself as death?

Does this woman scare you, Eugênio, after all the good moments you've shared, this woman you believe to be yours but has long ceased to feel she belongs to herself? Have you stopped trying to understand her in her moments of silence and harshness? Well, here I am, a bit skeptical, a bit tired, but still willing to tell you about an odd experience I carry with me, steeped in mist, my memories of it a labyrinth in the darkness, and please, don't ask me to be quiet, for telling you may be a way to shine a light on this forbidden, obscure, ghoulish territory. Besides, do you think we have the time to go on pretending nothing has happened? No one, Eugênio, not even you in all your selflessness, will be able to stop the things of this world from shattering, fading, growing moldy, tarnished. We know some things are born this way, broken, in tatters, and no amount of patching up can fix them.

Let me tell you, Eugênio, directly and honestly, a story I have kept carefully hidden for years. In the end, you may even ask what we have gained from it, what good has come from this confession of mine. I don't know if I will have a decent answer to give you. First of all, I must tell you I am not seeking your forgiveness. Or understanding or pity. I swear. I am not seeking anything. I just want you to know about a man who came into my life when you and I had been so inattentive, numbed by permanence, placidly living our lives as husband and wife. You shouldn't get upset. He is gone. He left without so much as a goodbye, without a trace. Did I love him? I don't know, Eugênio. I only know that when I met him, I was possessed by a tormented, obsessed feeling that embarrassed and incapacitated me like an infectious disease. Do you think he was extraordinary? A man among many, middle-aged, unattractive, skittish, lascivious. And this made my feelings grow stronger. How easy it was to love you, Eugênio, with your youth and kindness, your happy-boy eyes fixed on mine with steadfast sweetness. Sometimes I had the urge to hurt you, put to the test the trust I could see surfacing in your smile, undermine the strength I could feel in your love. And since then I had had an inkling, my dear, that one day I would do something to hurt you.

The first time I saw this man, he was about one hundred meters away, walking down the sidewalk by the seashore unsteadily, like a sleepwalker. I thought he might be a bit drunk. Instinctively, I stood in his field of vision but soon realized he couldn't see me because his eyes were vacant, like the eyes of someone looking within.

As soon as the distance grew smaller, I saw he was tall and wide, the skin on his face saggy, his beard and hair gray, his features stark and coarse. When he passed me, his eyes, puffy and bloodshot from tears, briefly gained a certain spark as they met mine, and he mumbled something to me, a single word, harsh and unintelligible, maybe an insult. I turned around to watch him walk away from me. And on an impulse, I decided to follow him.

Don't ask me why. You were always the one with the answers. Actually, you were the one who told me one day that we don't stumble on things; we are like marionettes at the hands of destiny. And so, Eugênio, based on your own words, I concluded that somehow, I was destined to meet that man, and nothing could stop me from finding him because all paths, no matter how tortuous, had been laid out so I could find my way to him.

Even though I stayed cautiously at a distance, I could sense the heat emanating from that body, more than heat, a tension, a magnetic force, a sort of calling that compelled me forward to him. If he had turned his head, he would have spotted me encroaching upon his night. And if he were to ask me what I wanted, I wouldn't be able to say, not even to myself. I could hear him, his labored breathing and his sobs, indifferent to the curiosity he was arousing in the passersby. I could almost touch him, his back and shoulders quivering to the rhythm of that pain that seduced me and repelled me at the same time. Why is it, Eugênio, that these undignified things have such a power to drag me in?

We walked for a good while, and although I wasn't tired, I began to worry I had strayed too much from where I had parked my car. At that time of evening, the flow of cars and pedestrians had dwindled to almost nothing. Suddenly, he stepped off the sidewalk and onto the sand. He made his way to the water in wide strides, shedding his shoes, then his shirt, then his pants in jerky, impetuous movements, which, under the half-light of a waning moon as his accomplice, I suspected were the penultimate gestures of a man determined to die. I pictured his body sprawled on the shore the next morning, an object of morbid curiosity to the early sea-bathers, his belly swollen, eyes open to the void, face hardened from so much water and salt.

He halted somewhere on the shore, the spot where the roar of the waves drowned out the distant pulsing of the city, where night became larger and deeper, more itself. As I stayed about six or seven meters behind and waited, a lump of nausea climbed up to my throat and almost cut my breathing. Perhaps he had been abandoned by the woman he loved, the last woman. Or his son had come down with a frightful disease that spelled certain death. Perhaps he had no house, no home, no family waiting for him, so that he was entirely free to do with his life as he pleased—walk aimlessly, sink into the sea, give up on life. He wouldn't be punishing or betraying anyone with his desperate gesture. Yet, he hesitated. What if there were something left to lean on?

I don't know how long it took, seconds or minutes, to overcome the embarrassment of having followed him and yell, my voice echoing over the rumble of the waves, "Sir!" I added softly, I think more to myself than to him, "Don't do it!"

He turned violently, and although I couldn't see him clearly, I divined in the dim light a face contorted in surprise and irritation. I wanted to run but didn't move, blood throbbing in my ears in piercing blows, while that big, naked, oneiric man, a god suddenly deprived of his powers approached me with the wavering stride of one who is not in a hurry, not even to die. Then he surprised me yet again. He sat not far from where I stood, his back to me, covered his face with his hands, and started to weep softly, like a boy nestled in his mother's lap crying over the loss of a pet.

What could explain my insistence on staying there, in that almost-darkness, listening to his sobs and sniffles, incautiously planted behind him, that stranger clinging to his own tragedy, as if it were the only thing that made sense in the world? Perhaps, Eugênio, I wanted to feel something that made me forget about my own world and the pointlessness of all my daily actions, something that would dispel my boredom with everything in my life, would take me away from myself. Life had to extend beyond my petty anguish, beyond your loving gaze smothering me with tenderness and benevolence and shoving me underground. Life had to be much more. Life could be that stranger's pain taking root in me, his vital signs pulsing in my flesh.

I sat next to him and touched his arm with the tips of my fingers. He smelled, his armpits sweaty from days of drifting about. He reeked of squalor and loneliness. My stomach jerked and jumped. Between curious and reverent, I continued to watch him. He kept his head tilted to one side, pretending to be unaware of my intruding presence. On his gloomy profile, I saw the marks of many years. He might be missing teeth. Surely other things must be missing from his life. Yes,

Eugênio, I was shaking with fear. You know how I had always been afraid of everything since childhood, people—dead or alive—animals, diseases. But I was shaking mostly with a strange euphoria. The proximity to that stranger aroused in me imprecise and contradictory emotions, sensations of hot and cold, attraction and repulsion, all of this growing within me and taking me over.

"I just wanted to help," I muttered, afraid he would notice in the tone of my voice, which sounded fake to me, how grotesque I felt at that moment. He guffawed, his body shook extravagantly, and in that feigned laugh there was perplexity and sarcasm. He turned his head and stared at me with glum concentration, panting, his breath ruined by alcohol. Then, he held me firmly by the arms and laid me down on the sand. I attempted no reaction. With one hand he held my wrists above my head and with the other he yanked off my underwear and placed his sex in mine, covering me with his huge body and taking me with ferocity and urgency. With each stab, his crazed eyes fixed on mine, he whispered, "bitch," and that mantra started seeping through me, penetrating my pores, bones, muscles, blood, sinking me into a deep, warm, dizzying space, while stars trembled above us. When he was done, he got up heavily, put on his clothes, and left.

For days, Eugênio, I was in a trance, searching my body for traces of that anonymous man's sweat, saliva, semen, smell, stroking the dents his mouth and teeth had left on my skin, wandering the streets near the shore, desperate with the thought I might never see him again, a maddening restlessness invading me like one of those powerful drugs that throw users into brutal, vertiginous sensations.

I would tell myself I only wanted to see him one more time. Preferably during the day, when his devastation would be displayed in its most minute details, and I could then come to my senses. Yet, when that happened and he recognized me and flashed me an arrogant grin, it was as if he were saying, *I knew you were looking for me, I was sure you would come.* It was only then that I noticed that his mouth, too big for such thin, tight lips, hadn't learned how to smile. My cheeks burned from shame and humiliation, but I didn't speak. I feared an improper or trivial word would put him out of my sight again. I feared he would reject me. He didn't say anything either, just looked at me with that distorted smile, turned around, and walked on. I breathed a sigh of relief that he didn't say something unpleasant to me. I simply followed him again, dragging myself behind him like a ridiculous appendage, a tail, which he accepted nonchalantly, as one accepts the inevitable.

This time, I walked with him to his windowless bedroom-and-bath in a poor area, to which I returned on many occasions in the next three or four months. As if in a gravitational field, I was sucked in, dragged, devoured by the black hole. And even when I looked at you, Eugênio, I wouldn't see you, and although in your company, truthfully it was there that I found myself, with him, or waiting for him by the locked door, sitting on the front steps, exposed to the neighbors' hostile or compassionate stares, while he drank himself to intoxication in some filthy bar, and then in a rage would crash into his own walls and punch them until his knuckles bled. I would hate him and curse him. Old, drunk, pathetic, how dare he leave me there, abandoned, a hostage to his indifference and selfishness? What else did he want? An acknowledgment of his power to make me come and to make me suffer? Did he want me to tear up my chest, pluck out my heart, and offer it to him, warm, bloody and throbbing, yelling so everyone could hear, *take, my lord, the breath of this life that now belongs to you*, as proof of my unconditional surrender and fervor?

Yes, Eugênio, I would feel indignant, outraged, the lowest of women and promise myself I would never see him again. Yet, the next day, there I was again in the ritual of waiting, corrupted by the desire to see him spring up with that hungry-wolf stare and lunge upon me and devour me and give me something like happiness if only for a moment, and then I would go back to things as they were, overwhelmed by a sense of helplessness and impossibility, filled with that man's absence. I was now completely at his mercy.

I was fascinated by his untamed, rude, insular nature, like a cactus, a desert. I was moved by that blood-thirsty rage, which gave him the air of a wounded, suspicious warrior, inseparable from his armor night and day, even for sleeping or lovemaking, in an endless skirmish with himself and with the dirty and perverse world of men, which he so despised.

I was scared to death he might not go back home, if one could call home the paltry room with damp walls and holes in the floor, where we took refuge to make love. I was afraid he would die. On many nights, after resorting to pills to try and get some sleep, while I was lying beside you, with your leg upon mine and your breath at my back, feeling safeguarded by your love, I was afraid he would jump into the sea or in front of a car. He kept a gun under his mattress. He could well make use of it to put a bullet through his chest. I would try to calm myself down from that state of anguish by telling myself I had been mistaken the night I met him, that all the time I had been following him, he had known about me and had cleverly led me to the beach because he had intended all along for things to unfold the way they eventually did. But I didn't really believe that. I would torture myself thinking that if he decided to try it again, I wouldn't be around to stop him. I would cry in self-pity. I would ask myself what would be more unbearable—life without you, Eugênio, or the loss of those days of flesh and agony.

I never knew what he did besides drinking, playing cards, and making love to me. Nor did I know the cause of that obsessive pain that tormented him and, I believed, had made him cry the day I met him. I burned with the desire to know his secrets, which I imagined were big and rough like him. Yet, there was no willingness on his part to share confidences. His silence protected him. As you know, Eugênio, words can make people vulnerable. Aren't words confirmation of the existence of the other, whom we so vehemently deny to avoid suffering?

Sometimes I would happen to hear him sing in the shower. He liked Noel Rosa tunes, the saddest ones. He had a nice voice, one that seemed not to come from within him, as if another man inhabited him, a pure and gentle man he adamantly rejected and moved me, my eyes brimming with tears.

Was I happy? How can you be so pure of heart, Eugênio? Those were gloomy, tormented, chaotic days. I never knew if I was going to see him today, tomorrow, or later. If I was going to have him again. I became obsessed, paranoid. With each encounter, I discovered a new omen of our separation. If he gave me a different look, I would see a hint of goodbye in it. The wait was constantly eating away at me. Uncertainty always tearing me up inside. And in all this emotional turmoil, I still had to deal with you. Yes, Eugênio, you continued to exist. You were always there, in bed, at the table, on the sofa, in the car, bewildered to watch my undeniable confusion. At any moment, you might confront me. And if you sent me away, where would I go without you, the only person who truly loved me? I wished I could keep you in a comfortable box, you and your violin, your pieces and scores, the moto perpetuo of your harmonious chords, your beautiful musical universe, and all the time necessary, even eternity, to live out our story fully. And I would tell you, *stay there, my darling, and wait for me without fear, because soon I will come back to your wholesome, clamoring love.*

What's the matter, you would ask, searching my eyes with mild suspicion. And I would stiffen with the fear you would find out, or worse, you already knew and were testing me, luring me into a trap. *Where have you been?* And I would make sure to tell you a convincing story, never without a measure of embarrassment. I am not sure you ever noticed. I remember you would change the subject to protect yourself, to preserve your innocence at all costs. Today I ask myself, what is plausible, Eugênio? If back then I had answered, I spend all afternoon rubbing myself on a degenerate man twice your age without a third of your virility, would you have believed me? Probably not. You would say I had lost my mind once and for all, or had developed a talent for jokes, and so would discard my most irrefutable truth.

I no longer undressed in front of you, afraid that the marks my lover's indecent, torturing love had imprinted on my skin would give me away. In the dark, wee hours of the night, you would seek me out, and I would allow myself to receive your gentle caresses, relieved not to have to fake enthusiasm, which had long deserted me. You didn't know, or didn't want to know, where I spent my afternoons, a place from which I would return never entirely satiated. Like a dog in heat, I wanted more, always more, but I didn't hunger for you, nor would any other man be able to quench that desire that pierced me through. There was a heart-sex, or a sex-heart, an anomalous, sharp organ penetrating every crevice of my flesh, Eugênio, pricking my scalp, clouding the pupils of my eyes, shining upon the roof of my mouth, hardening my nipples, setting my womb on fire. I hungered for him and him only. It was a wild, deep, anxious hunger. Surely in your eyes and in everyone else's, my lover was nothing but a tramp, a wretch, a man completely undone by life. How would you explain, then, that he was the only one who could carve out volcanos on my skin, sculpt moonlit nights in my mouth, swell to floods all my labial rivers?

It is true that I clung to his man with all the desperation and hope of a castaway. No, I didn't save myself, if that's what you're wondering. The bottom of my boat is splintered, and every now and then it lists under the force of unstable and mysterious underground currents, but the storm has lifted, and here with you, I am groping, trying to put some order to all these turbulent emotions, searching for a reconciliation with our fragile universe. Fragile and shattered, I know. But you must agree with me, it is possible and real.

Now that so many years have gone by, Eugênio, what I have just revealed seems as unreal to me as one of those stories we see in the movies. Or that we live out in a dream. An obscure and oppressive dream, almost a nightmare. An imprecise time punctuated only by God's whispers, an indeterminate place never touched by sunlight, towers and cathedrals in ruins, debris, bodies sniffed by frightful animals, swamps and wetlands, blood-red rivers, and the two of them, survivors of this beast we call life, doomed by a sorcerer's wicked spell to dance an illusory lover's tango to the end of time.

The Night of Alícia

A STREAM of light and The Ride of the Valkyries seep out from under the door. I ring the bell, and it is Alícia herself who greets me. I recognize immediately the husky voice, the turquoise eyes, the tight-lipped smile. She opens the door wide, shakes my hand, and soon I find myself in a large, well-lit living room. She offers me a seat on the sofa. While she pours me some whisky, I study her with curiosity. Her hips have grown rounder, and her breasts look fuller inside the bra I can make out under her see-through blouse. She is wearing pants rather than one of the flowery dresses of her youth, and her hair is so short she couldn't pull it back in a ponytail as she used to when I met her.

She hands me the glass and sits across from me, crossing the same legs that rattled me twenty-five years ago. Her face is so close to mine I can't help but see the inevitable lines around her eyes and smell the light fragrance of her perfume. She asks me about the family, our family. I tell her about my father's illness, the weddings and divorces of cousins she knew in their teen years, the births and deaths. Suddenly, I get the feeling she hears me with attention but not with enthusiasm. I stop talking.

On the turntable, Wagner comes to an end. A discomfiting silence follows. I try another topic, any topic, but words escape me—a man who always had a way with words. I feel uncomfortable, that's it. And, sadly, I realize the obvious: we have no familiarity with one another, nor will we have the time to build it. There is no willingness on her part.

She glances at her wristwatch. Perhaps she is waiting for someone. She had told me on the telephone, *come over and have dinner with us*. Where are her husband and children? As if reading my thoughts, she tells me her husband had gone on a trip, and she is expecting one of her sons and daughter-and-law, who will be joining us for dinner. I am quick to tell her I am not hungry and have nowhere else to be that night, so we can wait for them if she prefers.

Now she moves about the room while she pours another drink, I think a dry martini, and I take the opportunity to watch her more closely. She has her back to me, and I find nothing of the Alícia I had sought for so many years in all the women who have come in and out of my life, in the few I have loved. Only when she walks back to sit near me does something—I don't know what, the way she walks or brushes her hair away from her face—remind me of the other Alícia, the image I had framed in years of fantasies.

I was fourteen when Alícia came to spend summer vacation with us. She was about nineteen. Charming like most young women that age, but nothing more. Some of our older cousins started showering her with attention, but she barely paid them any mind. That is what I heard at home. I would see her at meals or when she left and came back from outings with the adults. She didn't seem very cheerful. Everyone said so. They would whisper about conflicts between her and my aunt and uncle—her parents—over a boyfriend she had left back where they lived. Such stories didn't matter to me at all until that one moment when I stepped into the room my grandmother had prepared for her to stay in those days.

The door wasn't locked, and I only meant to grab something or other I can't remember now. In fact, I didn't go in. I stood still at the doorway, first when I heard an indistinct murmuring, a moan, and then as I saw her half naked, stroking her breasts in front of the mirror. Alícia didn't see me, nor could she, absorbed as she was in the contemplation of her own body. I retreated into the hallway, feeling as if I had been punched violently in the stomach, and I could barely stand on my legs. I collapsed into an armchair in the living room, where the adults were talking, and from the way they were looking at me, I understood that such things are written all over those who experience them. They asked me if I was ill, and even though I said no, that is how I felt, suddenly feverish, with chills up and down my body, incapable of getting away and joining the other boys in their games. I was also terribly afraid my grandmother and the other adults in the family would find out about me, that they would suspect I had just seen my cousin's breasts.

It would be worse if my cousins, who would have given anything to be her boyfriend, were to guess what had happened to me by that bedroom door. I feared they would want to take away what belonged to me and to me only: the sublime vision of Alícia's breasts, firm, round, rosy, and of her nipples, which she was touching with the tips of her fingers, like the women I used to see in magazines, although I had never found in them the flame I had spied in the mirror—in Alícia's eyes.

Now, she is here right in front of me, telling me something and laughing easily, crinkling her nose. I, too, laugh to hide my temporary distraction. She is unlikely to have noticed. She doesn't know, never has known, of the days and nights I spent in my boyhood haunted by visions. To her, I am practically a stranger, an intruder, someone she feels obligated to welcome, listen to, and treat with courtesy because we are blood relatives. I doubt she has any memories of the shy, skinny boy who played ball in our grandmother's yard. There were many of us, cousins.

Truthfully, she is getting to know me today. Tomorrow, I will be forgotten once again, if I can even speak of forgetting when there is nothing to remember. Maybe even later today, after I am gone and Alícia has washed the glass from which I drank and the dishes and silverware I used to eat and has finally lain down to sleep, I will no longer exist. I will leave no trace of my presence, and there is nothing I can do about it. To tell her about those nights would be absurd and altogether pointless because the Alícia who stole away the sleep of my boyhood and filled my dreams with desire all these years, who is within me more than in the woman who now sits by me—that Alícia cannot be restored with words. What am I doing here anyway?

The telephone rings, and she walks across the room to answer it. I can't hear what she's saying, but she seems uncomfortable with what she hears. She hangs up and for a few seconds keeps her head down, suddenly distant, thoughtful. I ask her what has upset her. She tells me her son, who was supposed to join us for dinner, has just told her he can't make it. Alícia apologizes. She can't imagine how relieved I am to hear it. Relieved to be free from the looks and questions of a son and daughter-and-law who mean absolutely nothing to me. I would rather be alone with her, although I suspect that is not what she wishes, now that she looks at me and smiles weakly, a wrinkle forming across her forehead.

She asks me if I enjoy Piazolla while she disappears through a door without waiting for my reply. In her absence, I return to my Alícia, the Alícia from that magical scene in front of the mirror. The Alícia with the bared, full breasts, the strange spark in her eyes that I started to follow and to watch at all hours of day and night, fueled by a fantasy that was so particularly delicious. Because I could no longer sleep, I would spend my nights wandering around the house, lingering by her bedroom, analyzing the door handle, sliding my gaze through the keyhole.

Back then, I still didn't know women. What I knew about them I had been told by my older cousins. They would fondle their girlfriends and pay to lie with women who walked the streets downtown. Whores. That word alone, coming from one of my cousins, was enough to unnerve me. Then I would tell myself soon it would be my turn. I knew, or sort of knew, what was entailed, although I had a hunch things never went on exactly the way we thought they would. Looking smug and full of themselves, my cousins would ask me what I was waiting for. I didn't know. And they had their fun mocking me for that weakness. To tell the truth, I felt strangely threatened by that legendary universe of beautiful women, poised on impossibly high heels, with their warm and moist velvety sexes, which they said smelled of sea creatures.

Shall we eat now? Alícia is standing in front of me, the look on her face between puzzled and solicitous. I didn't see her approach. I smile in embarrassment, trying to regain my composure. She can't read my thoughts. My ghosts are not her ghosts. I tell her, yes, sure. To myself, I say I would rather enjoy her company a little longer. After the meal and the probable liqueur and coffee, I will be irreparably ready to leave, never to see her again.

She invites me to walk to the kitchen with her and take a stool by the window. Turns on the oven and leans on the counter. Starts to talk about her connection to music. She sounds more animated, as if the lament from the concertina in *Adiós Nonino*, which we hear now, had the power of pulling her out of her shell. She tells me about her time at the conservatory, the discipline her father demanded of her, hours and hours of study, the cramps in her fingers, and her sparse talent. After the marriage and kids, she got rid of the piano, and only then did she fall in love with music.

From the window on this fourteenth floor, I look out into the night. Above us, the mist. Below us, the blinking luminosity of headlights, traffic lights, neon signs. Loud and wild, this city of Alícia's, always on alert so as not to be devoured by its own self. Before lighting up a cigarette, I ask her if the smoke would bother her. No, she had been a smoker for eighteen years. Now she only drinks, occasionally. She keeps on talking, and I realize I haven't talked to a woman in her kitchen in many years. Nor even my wife. For the first time since I got here, I have a feeling of closeness, as if we were a couple with no trepidations or anxieties, absorbed in our familiarity, with all the time in the world to ourselves.

We are not a couple, nor do we have all the time in the world. Soon I will be leaving. What matters is each contraction of Alícia's face, each movement of her body, each attempted gesture, each uttered word. I won't have her near me tomorrow or after. I won't be back to sit here and listen to her as she talks about her likes and dislikes. No missteps or betrayals will ever happen between us. Or moments of indifference or sarcasm. We will never hurt each other. We will always be these two people—I and the Alícia of here and now.

She leads the conversation. I don't know much about the topic, but I think I have some musical sensibilities. I tell her so, and she nods in agreement, as if she knew me well or simply believed me. I tell her of my preference for Bach, and she winks at me in complicity. We toast to the night and to the dish which has just come out of the oven.

Before we take our places at the table, Alícia leaves me alone again. To change the record, I assume. I am correct. She comes back smiling deliciously, lulled by the drinks and Albinoni's *Adagio*. I start to feel a bit inebriated after the four whiskies I have had, enough to make life fabulous and all people infinitely generous, to redeem me of all my failures, to make time and death forgettable.

Now Alícia tells me in detail how she prepared our dinner. I try to pay attention and pretend her cooking skills interest me. I will never forget that fish must have firm flesh, like salmon, and be seasoned with salt, pepper, lime, and vodka. Otherwise, I chew, look at her from time to time, and nod in approval while memory insists on pulling me back to her, to the Alícia that does not fit into this evening, too small for the size of my dream.

The desire to see Alícia's breasts again, or rather to watch her stroking them, led me to plan a sure-fire way to spy on her without raising the suspicions of the others in the house. Her bed faced the glass window that opened up to the garden. If I wished, I could sneak into the room while she was out and place the curtain in such a way that it would stay open only a bit and not enough for Alícia to think of closing it before going to bed. She had no idea what that arrangement would afford me.

Every night, after everyone had gone to bed, I would hide in the garden under Alícia's bedroom window. From where I stood, I could only see her lying down or sitting on her bed. I would stand there for hours, watching her while she remained still, looking at some undefined spot on the ceiling or twirling her hair with the tips of her fingers, then turned on her stomach with her head buried on the pillow and fell asleep, always well covered by her bedsheets.

Once I saw her crying and left my hideout feeling terribly guilty, afraid I might have caused those tears, as if she could guess I was on the other side of the window, crouched over the jasmine bush, under the cover of darkness, unworthy of her greeting me the next morning. However, now lying in my own bed and feeling like a wimp, I decided to go back to my stakeout and did so the very next night.

That was the night. I was there by Alícia's bedroom window when I saw her get up, stand by the foot of the bed, and start undressing slowly, gracefully, bathed in the pastel lamp light as if she were performing for a voyeuristic lover, and I saw her lie down, open her thighs wide, and touch the space between, a space no longer hidden, the red and tumescent sex which for a moment looked like one of those birds just hatched out of their little eggs we used to steal from the nests only to see them die on our hands hours later.

First she touched herself gently, then more and more vigorously, and while she did so, she would say something I couldn't hear, but from the movement of her lips I deduced it was a repetition, the same words murmured incessantly, words that seemed so hot and intense that I had the feeling I was being dragged into her body, melting like ice cream in the sun, her body twisting and preventing me from seeing her face for a moment, until she doubled over and, as if hit by an electric charge, stretched out so much I thought she might break. Then, she lay still and closed her eyes. I stepped away and wandered around the garden, stumbling, devastated by that vision which split my life into two: before and after Alícia's climax.

Now we are sitting across from each other, and she has no idea how much of that distant night I carry with me. She doesn't know how these memories have followed me throughout my life, although they become less precise as time goes by. Memory betrays us, and some of the images I have of those nights have become diluted or vanished altogether amidst so many others. But like a song one hears many times early in life, a song from mother to child, repeated on seemingly endless nights, partly forgotten but surviving as an inner solfege that is not silenced or erased—that is how the memory of a single one of Alícia's nights stayed within me.

It is late. She jokes around, light-hearted, relaxed. She offers me some coffee, and I politely decline. There is nothing else to wait for. Actually, I still don't know what I expected to find before I got here, if I actually expected anything. In the disarray of my fantasies, Alícia never failed me. As a reality, I know now she will not suffice. Why prolong this night any further if I have Alícia's night, the greatest night, inside of me?

As I say goodnight, I feel melancholy. Frustrated perhaps. She walks me to the elevator. I tell her I will be leaving town the next morning, and she looks at me with her light, clear, kind eyes, smiles her tight-lipped smile, shakes my hand, and wishes me a nice trip back.

The Passenger

THAT THURSDAY, I left the clinic early and had three beers at the corner bar before calling Una. She was already waiting for me, as usual. We were in the habit of going out once a week to eat at a good restaurant and talk a little outside of our home. She would always be more light-hearted and cheerful on those nights, the way she used to be when we first met.

On the telephone, I told her I was famished and would be home in half an hour for a quick shower. As soon as I got in the car, it started to sprinkle, and traffic became slower and more exasperating. I turned on the radio to relax and, as I remember it, Janis Joplin was singing *Summertime*, my wife's favorite song.

Then, the young woman showed up. I had stopped almost on top of the pedestrian crossing and was waiting for the green light so I could take off again when she crossed the street and suddenly stopped in front of my car, narrowing her eyes as if trying to determine who I was. I had been absorbed by the fine rain running down the windshield between the back-and-forth of the wipers when I saw her, a small figure standing very straight, indifferent to the imminent light change and to the others crossing the street.

When the light turned green, I shined my bright beams at her. But instead of moving out of the way, she came towards me waving, signaling to me that I should wait for her. And before I could figure out what she wanted, the passenger door opened and she hopped into the car, a husky voice issuing the command, *Go, now!*

For a few seconds I couldn't move, too stunned and outraged to react. Loud honking blasted behind me, demanding, as she did, that I start off now. I complied, speechless, attentive to the slightest movements to my right. She didn't seem to be armed and had even leaned her head back on the rest, so still that for a moment I thought she had fallen asleep, which would be far too odd for a robber or even a hitchhiker.

Four or five blocks ahead, I decided to ask where I should drop her off, but much to my annoyance, she didn't reply. She didn't even seem to have heard me. I looked at her from the corner of my eyes, irritated with her intrusion and nerve. Although she didn't look it, she definitely could only be insane. Neither fat nor thin, the firm thighs exposed by the skirt that had hiked up when she sat down, the disheveled hair dripping down her high school girl profile. There was something between innocence and malice on her young and yet weathered face, marked by something other than wrinkles or expression lines, something more damaging, like a painful experience perhaps.

I asked her what she wanted from me, and looking at me with thick lashes and a slightly wandering eye, she said, *I want you to take me home and stay with me, forever this time.*

I smiled, trying to hide my discomfort. How could she want me if she didn't know me, if she had never seen me before? A woman from the streets, drunk, high, crazy, I don't know what, not even pretty. That was just my luck. I no longer knew how to deal with that kind of situation. I thought back to a time before I got married, when it was forbidden to squander any opportunity to bed girls who made themselves available, at just the right beat of urgency and anonymity.

Now, there was Una. And I could picture her at that moment in front of the mirror in our bathroom, getting dressed or putting on make-up, getting ready for our evening together. If I got home late, I knew she would ask questions and I would end up telling her about the stranger who had accosted me in traffic and had installed herself in my car without permission, and until she could make something out of this incident, if that were even possible, we would both have lost any interest in going out and having fun.

I looked at the stranger beside me again as I drove down the wide road that smelled of wet asphalt. Her face and neck were so white. Her fine hair came down to her shoulders and could be red or light brown, I didn't know and wouldn't know because it was wet and there was no time for it to dry, there was no time for certainties. Her hands, she wringed restlessly. Around her eyes, the mascara ran down in smudges, diluted by the rain. No, that woman definitely didn't please me. But something about her was unsettling to me.

Perhaps in a different time, when I was still single, I could have taken her to some room or even her own bed, as she had proposed herself, to do as she wished, to love her as a good man would. I wasn't sure if she would accept my money. A prostitute wouldn't behave that way, insolent, cold. I thought, then, that she might have gotten me mixed up with someone, but I didn't dare ask her. I decided to wait, even though I couldn't afford to. Right at that moment, Una would be ready, or almost ready, so beautiful that she still stoked the fire of my masculinity, even after eighteen years of marriage.

Would it be possible to meet up some other time?, I asked without facing her, and suddenly I felt annoyed at the impossibility of having her that night. The most absurd part is that she hadn't impressed me as a woman. It wasn't a matter of desire. Something else was compelling me to keep up that game. That was extremely inconvenient, not to mention incomprehensible, to me.

However, she wasn't offended by my refusal. She started to curl up and slide next to me, her gaze warm, full of hooks that grabbed me and pulled me towards her, and touched my sex firmly but gently, sure of what she was doing, and at that moment I intuited I was not going to get rid of her, not as easily as I thought, because whatever it was—an impulse, poor judgment, insanity—it was out of my control.

I pulled over to the sidewalk and turned off the engine and my cell phone. I didn't want Una to ask me any questions right then. I would get flustered in my explanations, and she certainly would detect the lie. She had that gift. Or perhaps I wasn't good at lying to her. I didn't want to ruin our evening, but it was already lost. I wouldn't feel comfortable, nor would I be able to bring a single smile to her face with that stranger lodged inside me. It would be a slow, painful night: Una wanting to know, asking me relentlessly about what had happened, while I conjured disjointed excuses until she became upset and said she wanted to go home, without touching her food.

The woman sat back in her seat and lowered the window, and now she was looking out into the night. I watched her at length. She was no longer a girl. Had a common face. Pale skin, thin lips and nose. Nothing alluring. No. There was nothing we should be doing together. There was nothing I could say to her or she to me. But there we were, side by side, waiting for something, though I didn't know what. Not yet.

I told her, then, that I wanted her to promise me I would see her again. That evening I had to be somewhere and couldn't postpone it, I was already late, I asked her to please understand, some other time, tomorrow even, in the afternoon, I would cancel a few appointments, I would go anywhere she wanted.

She started to laugh. An easy, high-pitched laugh like that of a child. She laughed so hard she bent forward, her hair dripping on her thighs, her back exposed in the halter top. Ill at ease, I smiled too and asked why she was laughing. She looked at me as she calmed down and dried her tears, then she let herself fall into my arms again. Whether she was a crazy woman or a tramp, I didn't care, I wanted her, I was sure of it, and that growing, pressing, brutish desire confirmed itself in my body, to my own astonishment.

I squeezed her in one full-body caress, buried my nose in her lemon-grass scented hair, groped her silky thighs, kissed her hard on the neck, ears, mouth, eyes. Una had told me we only kiss the eyes of the one we love.

There was barely anyone walking around, and the cars were zooming by. Soon she made herself small, warm and comfortable on my lap, and we moved on to more intimate caresses, my body as aroused as if she were my first woman. I couldn't believe that was happening to me, after so many years of placid love with Una, of warm kisses, repeated words and images, gentle touches, and satisfaction.

In an instant, I was inside the stranger. And she was saying something, her breathing hard, her voice breaking up, begging, while I tried to understand her: *please, do it the way I like it, the way we always did it.* I didn't want to think of anything, not then, but everything led me to believe that I must look like another man, that was it, that had to be it, someone she used to sleep with, who knew her well in her lovemaking preferences. But not even that thought weakened my desire to remain where I was. Then, she pushed me abruptly away and hopped on to the passenger seat, covering her breasts with her top and shaking her head, looking dejected.

Confused, I asked her what had happened, what I had done wrong, why she had changed so unexpectedly. She answered with another question. She wanted to know why I had abandoned her and our son, how I had been able to forget everything, our love and all the many years we had lived together.

I burst out laughing, frustrated, startled, and incredulous. That was a bad joke, and it had to end right that minute. I had missed my whole evening with Una, I would have to give her an explanation, come up with a lie, not to mention the hassle of putting up with her bad mood for days, how dumb to sit there, having sex with an insane woman, out in the street, like a reckless teenager. What was wrong with me? Was that tramp's madness contagious? No. Then, it was a simple matter. All I had to do was push her out of my car, go on home, and try to forget the whole incident that had ruined my evening.

I took a deep breath. I wanted to project the calm I no longer felt when I asked her who she thought I was and where she thought she knew me from. I obviously didn't expect a sensible answer, but if she kept up that charade, I would leave her right there. I was also no longer worried about how she would react. She could even hurt me if she wished, if she had a weapon in her purse. But she didn't move. She only burst into tears, her face hidden in her hands, and muttered words that made no sense, filled with a sadness that made her look smaller and more miserable.

I looked down and waited. I had no intention of insulting her, nor would I hurt her. I wanted her to leave without my having to drag her out of the car. But while I heard her sob and thought of a way to untangle myself from her and from that unprecedented situation, I was taken with a strange sensation, a sort of compassion for myself, as if her tears were being shed for me, and it took me a while to understand that I actually didn't want to leave her, I wanted her very much, even thought that obscure and inconsequential desire tormented me. I had a wife, a family, people who loved and respected me. Since I had met Una, I had always avoided any involvement with other women. And now this one had shown up, out of thin air, offering herself to me, telling me she was mine, when I had no clue who she was.

I wanted to give her one last chance. No, that is not true. It was my last chance. I took her hand and asked her to please stop crying and tell me where she wanted to go, I was exhausted, wanted to get back home, have dinner, go to bed. We would talk some other time. Her wet glaze clung to mine, and the pain I saw floating in her eyes took my breath away, a pain that I could chase away simply by taking her home and loving her, as she had asked me, until she felt at peace and I would be able, then, to resume my own life.

What are you talking about? Pretending you don't know who I am, who we are? She spoke in a mocking tone, her voice shrill, her eyes suddenly dry and cruel. I didn't know what to do. I was too rattled to make any kind of decision. On impulse, I told her to get out of the car, to go away, or I would drag her out myself. And I immediately regretted saying it. How could I lay eyes on that woman, with no name and no history but in possession of my love without my ever knowing it, and not relent? She had so taken me over—and that frightened me— that all I wanted to do was get rid of Una, of all my engagements and conventions, be free to devote myself to her, to her love and madness. Maybe she was right. Maybe I didn't really know who I was. Didn't know anymore. At that moment, my life seemed to me like a great lie. And I, the greatest bluff.

She rummaged through her purse, took out a photograph, and handed it to me without a word. I turned on the top light to see it better. I recognized right away the shirt Una gave me for one of my birthdays. Soon, I spotted the scar on the chin, and on the right hand a ring my father gave to me. That was me, caught right next to the woman and a pinkish baby with his single-tooth smile. In the background, ferns and a cat stretching on a stone wall. The family posing in their garden.

Fear. Of her and of myself. A ringing in my ears, my saliva growing thick, nausea. And my heart trying to catch its beat. If I had at least a glimmer of memory. . . But what was there to remember? No. I couldn't be. It was another man, and the shirt was just a coincidence. What about the scar, the result of a fall from a horse in my childhood? The distinctive ring, a family jewel, a graduation gift from my father? Why was I being robbed of myself, oh God?

I looked at her with alarm. She had brought me death. If I wished, I could throw her out into the street, kick her away from me like a flea-infested dog, and hurry home to Una, to the comfort of my predictable love, to the realm of our identical nights. And yet, I wanted to go back to that place where I had never been, to the life of a woman who was a stranger to me.

I took her there, to the place where she insisted we lived together—I, she, and the baby from the photograph. It was a two-story house with a hammock on the porch, stained glass windows, bougainvillea in the garden, fruit trees in the yard. Once, many years ago, I had dreamed of living in a house like that, but Una convinced me to buy an apartment instead.

I knew where to find the key to the front door—she didn't have to tell me where it was—hidden in the gazebo. I wasn't a stranger after all. And that is where I belonged. I had been pushed into the immensity of the dream or nightmare of a woman who had crashed into my night with her extraordinary and undoubtable love, a love that attracted me as much as it repulsed me.

In the living room, other photographs of a common history, my favorite records and books, and on some of them, my signature. All around the house, personal objects redolent of a familiar scent—mine.

As we walked into the bedroom, a boy who apparently had just woken up opened his eyes wide, ran towards me, and threw his arms around my neck, squealing with excitement, as children do when they see their parents.

I threw up until I fell hollow. I felt as though I had been smashed with a pickaxe, pieces of me floating in a body I was no longer sure I could call mine. The woman came to me, cleaned me up, and helped me lie in the bed where we had made the baby at a time I had never fathomed. She smiled, and how pretty she looked then. Her facial features were relaxing. I wanted to tell her about that beauty just revealed to me, but before I could do so, and before I could make love to her, I fell asleep.

Sunflowers in Hell

ON THE day we buried Arturo, the sky was a cloudless blue. As we walked from the funeral home to the cemetery, a great blazing sun weighed mercilessly on our heads, and a suffocating heat lifted off the asphalt. My mouth was dry, my head hollow, and my stomach in knots. Where my heart had been was a giant thorn, and I could hardly breathe. My sons walked by my side, their eyes low, their steps dragging on. It was hard to face them. They still had no idea what had happened to their father. I didn't want anyone to tell them. Not at that moment. That I knew how it all had come to pass was hard enough. If I had been offered the choice of never finding out, I would have taken it. But I knew, I knew, and that was as unbearable as the certainty that I would never have Arturo again.

Before they lowered the coffin and laid it at the bottom of the grave, I signaled to them that I wanted to see him one last time. They lifted the heavy lid, and I leaned over the carnation-covered body. I squeezed his cold hands, held my face close to his, and waited. If at that moment he had taken another breath, I would have forgiven him. No. He was no longer there. And what was left of him would soon decay and feed the worms. Off Arturo went, to close the circle, join the cosmos. That stranger was my departed. All his untimely death had left me was a legacy of fear, pain, and confusion.

The previous night, a few minutes before the body arrived, I had learned Arturo was not alone when he had the heart attack. He and this other person, probably a woman, had been in his car, which was found in a deserted area in the outskirts of town almost two days after Arturo went missing. Inside the car, the police had found signs of that anonymous presence. Bottles of wine, two of them empty, a folder with hand-written poems, hair that didn't belong to Arturo, and a handkerchief stained with sperm.

It is true that people despise the betrayed more than the betrayer. On the days following Arturo's burial, I didn't take well the sympathy visits, the compassionate gazes, the comments whispered behind my back. When the impact of those first weeks had lessened, however, people started forgetting about us, about me and my sons, which is natural, and it was only then that Arturo's absence and the incomprehensibility of his behavior settled intensely within me. I had the sensation I was constantly tumbling down a bottomless pit, completely uprooted, stupefied by resentment, abandonment, and impotence. I was stunned that everything else could keep going on without my intervention, that I knew less than I had ever known about everything, that all my certainties were crumbling down with me.

A month later, after the memorial, I decided to go see the place where Arturo had spent his last hours. I went there that day and many times after. I walked down the same trail the lovers had followed, trod the same ground covered by that other person, the one who abandoned him, no doubt to avoid being identified.

I spent whole afternoons completely still, lying in the shade of a fig tree, the only tree within several kilometers, where he had parked his car that summer morning to avoid the scrutiny of others. Right there he had loved the woman I knew nothing about, the stranger who had left him all alone at the time of his death. I had been told that near the car, on the passenger's side, the footprints clearly suggested that someone had fled in a hurry, someone who in all likelihood had panicked at the heart attack that ended my husband's life and for obvious reasons didn't want to be seen by his family and friends.

Every day, awake or asleep, I would dream of the woman in whose arms Arturo had been shortly before he left us. A colleague from his department? Someone he used to talk to about the poetry of Keats, the music of Gershwin, the films of Visconti? Perhaps a young and devoted student, who had assisted him in his research, who revered him for his integrity and intelligence? Or a prostitute, an escort, ready to welcome him, picked up in some alley and brought to that place for the fleeting satisfaction of his masculinity?

Whoever she was, I was sure she had impressed him. Reserved and cautious, scrupulous to the extreme, Arturo wouldn't have taken such a risk for a meaningless fling. I would conjure up images where the lover always appeared as master of his desire and passion, a beautiful, powerful, and sexy woman, imprecise in her seven veils, astutely seductive. I also imagined her free from conventionalities and limitations, sure of herself, defiant, willing to know and be known, blaze new trails, aware that no one belongs to anyone, that nothing is forever.

They must have met once or twice a week and made love in the car or some illicit room, where time was limited and, certainly for Arturo, growing insufficient. He wanted more, and yet, there was the family, our sons and I, denying him his dream, stopping him from experiencing fully the magic of that encounter.

The truth is, for some time he had been giving me indications of his double life. In recent months, I had been awakened by the sounds coming from him. He would grind his teeth hard, as if he were going to break them. I would also find him roaming the house and smoking compulsively in the middle of the night.

I know now how adamantly I avoided acknowledging anything that might threaten our life as a couple, throwing it into disarray at that point, when we had lived together for more than twenty years. Only now do I understand how very distant I had kept from Arturo's suffering. I thought the small resentments collected over those many years would never stop us from appreciating the certainty of our lives together with our sons, secure in the comfort of repetition, in the conviction that we were fulfilling sufficiently our roles as parents and partners. There were moments of intolerance, I admit, of boredom and dissatisfaction, of glowering and harsh words, but we were alive—weren't we?—and above all we loved each other.

A stroll on a sunny morning, a remote refuge, an obscure love, a faltering heart. Arturo was gone. The loss I experienced was twofold—the man I loved and my own identity.

Who was going to ask me at the end of each day, *hey, girl, how are things going?* With whom would I now share the two bottles of red wine on Friday nights, when the boys were asleep and we would sit out on the porch, inebriated by the sounds of the surf breaking on the shore and the sea breeze on our faces, in our customary conversation of few words?

If only I hadn't believed so firmly that emotionally mature and responsible men like Arturo didn't get involved with people outside their marriage... If I hadn't put on that armor of certainty that I knew him too well, that he had long lost the ability to surprise me. . . If I had paid closer attention to his words and his silence. . . If I had grasped the importance of what is not uttered, of what inhabits the caves of our souls, ticking bombs with the power to destroy everything around us. If, if, if! God! How could I ignore the look in his eyes, like a cornered animal, the agony behind the silence, the constant obsessions, the boredom even with his books and classes? Clearly his academic activities no longer provided relief from the agony of feeling torn, the torture of having to lie. Arturo, who had always prized honesty so highly! But at that moment, what would the truth have cost him? Leaving me or leaving her? One was his reality, a serene affection. The other, his fantasy, a transgression. He had the plain, and he had the cliff. Either option was too high a price to pay. Better to leave things as they were. Let destiny make that choice. Then, the quotidian had become a Russian roulette of sorts, the cylinder spinning right there, on his skin, his ear, his stomach, his heart. At any moment, the blast. My poor Arturo. . . I didn't understand then that life, transitory and imperfect, shows no mercy for those who settle into themselves and crush with their presumptuous paws those who hesitate for fear of disruption and change.

At first I didn't think it was fair to ask him questions, and I had never had a knack for interrogations or conflict anyway. Besides, I didn't see any reason to be suspicious. I would tell myself he had always lived in his shell, which was charming, but he was also honest and loyal. I couldn't doubt his life revolved around me and our sons, and that together we were safe from any harm—anything that could throw off our rhythm, expose us, kick us out of our bunker.

Arturo was also in the habit of going for solitary walks along the shore and isolating himself inside our own home, in the office, to listen to his music, prepare his classes, or simply be by himself. And yet, he was the kindest, most affectionate man I knew. With his strong hands, he could fix things that were broken at home and massage my shoulders gently when I was tense. He would listen to the boys patiently and advise or reprimand them wisely, with his firm and measured professor's voice.

And then one time, a few months before his death, I told him we needed to talk, and like a child caught in mischief, he broke down in convulsive sobs. When I asked him why he was crying, he threw himself in my arms and cried harder. At that moment, I felt things were getting out of control, and our fishbowl of a life, its water crystalline for so many years, was turning cloudy. And if we didn't address it, we would soon find ourselves instead adrift in a rough sea. Or perhaps our fishbowl had already turned into a swamp or a quicksand pit?

Something was eating away at Arturo and undermining our relationship. Something with mandibles, tentacles, sharp claws, and slimy eyes. But my fear may have been greater than his. What existed out there, outside of our world, didn't interest me. And so I too was cheating when I asked him to go see a doctor, get his blood pressure and his fat and sugar levels checked, when I asked him to take care of himself so I could have him forever, healthy, quotidian, so mine, knowing all the while that he was not ill. He would promise to schedule an appointment with a heart specialist, and shortly afterward he would forget about it. Arturo had forgotten to take care of himself. What he could not help remembering was that new love.

I had to meet her, look her in the eye, touch her, hear her. I had to assure myself of her existence, cleanse myself of that deep wound. She had left a single trace behind: *Sunflowers in Hell*. That was the title of the collection of poems found upon Arturo's death. I could smell her on those pages, thirty or so, written by hand on loose sheets of paper, which she had left in the back seat in her hurry to get away. She had surely brought them along so my husband could appraise them. It seems there had been no time for that because he hadn't made any notes on the margins, the way he used to when he evaluated his students' writing.

I took *Sunflowers in Hell* to an expert I knew. I told him I had found them in Arturo's desk and would like to return them to the author, as they seemed to be the originals, but unfortunately there had been no identifying information. Or perhaps they had been copies of someone else's work—someone, mediocre or great, known in the field but unknown to me.

I had read those poems dozens of times but had no idea of their merit. They seemed too serious, hermetic, arrogant. What I had hoped in reality was that they would tell me the history of the love affair. The professor took the poems and promised he would call me as soon as he had finished reading them. When he came over a few days later, he sounded quite enthusiastic. I would have been so pleased to hear these were poems by a minor writer. No. They were tremendously beautiful, wild, anti-academic, and he too would love to meet the author of such powerful, original poems.

One day, some years ago, Arturo stated, in one of his lectures on the literary universe, that among all human beings, artists were the only ones who could save themselves from banality because of their god-like energy, because they carried within themselves the seeds of a greater conscience, because they had the ability to grow empty and put their souls to the service of creation. And now, there she was. A scribbler of verse had been able to yank him out of our cocoon. Besides physical intimacy, they shared a passion for words, for the power they have to give shape to the world.

I was devastated. I thanked the professor and told him I hadn't lost hope that, although it was unlikely, one day whoever had written those poems would turn up and claim them. He asked if he could keep some of the poems. He knew many people in the field—writers, critics, artists. Who knows? He might one day have the pleasure of finding himself face to face with the poet who had so moved him.

Months went by. I told myself every day that I would not go back to the site of the tragedy, but like a sleepwalker or guided by occult forces, once again there was I, or rather a part of me that was still alive, imprisoned by the same morbid thoughts, interrogating and torturing me, trying to comprehend, to offer me the possibility of forgiveness.

Away from that place, there was only being nowhere. Even in my own home, I felt I was no more than a guest. I could barely get out of bed, stuffed full of pills to sleep, pills to wake up. It pained my sons to witness my apathy, but I was unable to break the cycle. That was more harrowing, crueller than anything I had ever faced.

No one ever walked by the spot where Arturo had chosen to be alone with his love. Every now and then, an airplane or flock of egrets would fly across the sky. Some animals grazed in the distance, white and slow, unaware of their own existence, of death and loneliness. As I looked on, I was filled with the desire to be one of them, non-thinking, free of any wounds to the soul.

What I had, then, were those empty afternoons, the flatness of a blue or grayish sky overhead, and the soft rustling of the wind through the leaves of the fig tree. The quiet gave me the feeling I was disintegrating, becoming shreds of myself, a self without Arturo, sinking in the tangle of roots. I would close my eyes and feel the pulsing of underground waters, the smell of the earth, its deep breathing underneath my body. I felt temporarily pacified but would soon go back to ruminating over a history that wasn't mine because I had been irrevocably pushed away from it. I could even hear the laughter, the voices, the moaning, feel the heat of the bodies in their embrace, smell the acrid and exciting odor of love. Chills ran through my arms and legs as I dived into that dark river with no edges and no bottom: my pain.

My life was in limbo, and I could think of only one way to pull myself out of it: to meet the woman Arturo had fallen in love with before he died. There were nights when I would dream of her, but I could never see her face because her back was always turned to me, and I would try to reach her, but she would escape me. I would beg her to wait, tell her I had to see her, but she couldn't hear me, so she would move on and fade away. One time, though, she turned towards me, and her face was Arturo's.

All I had to do was summon his memory, and a vague image of the woman would attach itself to me. It was part of what I called the construction of my mourning. Although I was aware of how obsessive and degrading that was, and of how it allowed me to justify a loss I was unable to process,

I was certain all I had to do was meet her, and things would go back to normal, and I would be healed. I was putting what little energy I had left into finding a ghost. And I knew full well ghosts play tricks, leap out of the darkness, laugh at our fears and doubts, vaporize into nothing, and make us crazy. Where was that going to lead me?

When I had almost lost hope that someone would show up in search of the poems, a man called. He said he knew the professor and the author of the poems, and that person was willing to meet me. Without hesitation, I asked him to come by the apartment later that afternoon. As soon as I hung up, I felt the onset of nausea, dizziness, and cold sweats. I had waited for that moment for months, and now it all seemed senseless.

I had trouble getting up when the bell rang. My legs shook, and my heart throbbed throughout my body. I was overwhelmed when I opened the door and faced the young, skinny man before me. He greeted me in a neutral tone. I thought that at the last minute Arturo's lover had backed out and sent an intermediary in her place, someone she trusted, a brother maybe, or a friend. So she didn't have the courage to confront me. Disappointed, I invited him in. He hesitated a bit by the door, then followed me to the sofa and sat by my side. I examined him with some embarrassment. He was wearing jeans and worn-out sneakers. He was probably a little over twenty-five years old. He rubbed his hands on his pants repeatedly, as if to dry palms that kept getting wet, his eyes averting mine.

In the silence that followed, the discomfort grew immensely. I felt it would be useless under the circumstances to try to have a conversation with anyone other than the woman. I had planned in my head the questions I was going to ask and even the appropriate intonation with which to ask them. But I had been faced with the unexpected, and I couldn't sit there forever, next to that stranger. Waiting for what?

I got straight to the point. He blushed intensely and mumbled something or other when I asked him why she hadn't come. At that moment, I intuited what I was to learn momentarily. At once, my legs grew slack, and my head turned into a cauldron bubbling with ideas, all muddled and tangled, while I tried in vain to make sense of them, fear throbbing in my veins with the cruelty of magma. At last, I heard myself ask, *so you were the one with Arturo?*

He looked at me with pain in his eyes and confirmed with a slight nod of his head. He then got up abruptly, whispered a *forgive me*, and darted out of the apartment, leaving me alone with my stupor and exhaustion. On an impulse, I ran after him but ended up turning back before reaching the elevator. That was no longer necessary. It was all over, and I was waking up from a long nightmare.

On the table, I spotted the folder that held the poems, whose author had left before I had the chance to tell him how much his incomprehensible lines had haunted me.

The Man Who
Came from a Dream

FROM WHERE she was, in the center of a dilapidated ware-house and with no idea how or why she found herself there, Dalila spotted with vague distress a wooden gate and a beam of sunlight filtered through its slats. So, it was day, although inside everything was blanketed in shadows. There were crates, dust, and spiderwebs everywhere.

A rat scurried by her and disappeared into a pile of sacks. She imagined dozens of those repugnant creatures hiding in there. She wanted to get up and run, but her feet felt as if tied up in chains. She closed her eyes and tried to remember what had happened before she got to that place. But her memory had turned into a black hole, affording no trace of a past, as if she hadn't existed until then.

She heard a familiar sound, a rattle, like a child's toy. Opening her eyes wide in the dim light, she saw a snake coiled up about three or four meters away, its head in an arc above the rest of the body, moving its tail and tongue rapidly toward her. Still and terrified, Dalila started to cry softly, swallowing her sobs out of fear the creature might hear her and pounce, killing her in a single and treacherous strike.

She wanted to free herself from that moment, put an end to the uncanny sway of that absurd situation and her powerlessness to fight it, but whom could she ask for help if the only sounds of living things were the rodents' squeaks and the pigeons' cooing on the tin roof?

Suddenly, the snake relaxed its head, uncoiled itself, and slithered away, disappearing among the crates, as if it had heard a call. Dalila tried to move once more, but her legs didn't respond. She wriggled painfully across the cement floor and realized the pointlessness of her attempt. She wouldn't have the strength to reach the exit. Her body was failing her, locked in place for reasons beyond her comprehension. Besides, the snake could come back, perhaps it was only waiting in its hideout for the best time to attack. It was clear she would only escape that menace if someone came to take her away. Someone who might be walking by the abandoned warehouse and heard her scream. She wasn't alone in the world. Outside, life went on. It didn't matter how she had come to be a prisoner there. It mattered how she was going to get out. Now!

She heard a noise close to her. She lifted her head and saw him. Inside the shadows, a pair of eyes and a dot of light at the end of a cigarette. But instead of cheering up at the sight of her would-be rescuer, Dalila felt frightened. Where had he come from if the gate hadn't been opened? He had always been there, then, watching her, having fun at her expense, mocking her for being a prisoner. That was the feeling, of being prisoner to something she knew was obscure and imperative, an undefined mass crushing her. A prisoner to that spectator come out of nowhere.

She saw the man move towards her with irregular steps, dragging one leg. She saw him stand in front of her for a while, blowing cigarette smoke in her face. He then put out his hand and helped her up, his bottomless-pit gaze slashing her like a whip. Dalila stepped back and was so dizzy she almost fell backward. The man grabbed her suddenly and squeezed her against his body, rubbing on her face his bony, sparsely bearded cheek. She shuddered at the stench emanating from him and tried to push him away, but he held her firmly without hurting her, overpowering her without effort.

What do you want, Dalila whispered imploringly. In response, silence, his eyes constantly on her, dragging her to a spot devoid of memories of terror or pain. It wasn't enough to close her eyes to lose that dizziness. The man wasn't only in his own body and in his own gaze. He seemed to manifest rather in a state of being and feeling, a record attached to Dalila, a suction pump sliding under her eyelids and claiming her.

She became aware immediately that she was at the mercy of that stranger and whatever he wished, whatever he wanted from her, there was nothing she could do to stop him, she was sure, because she had no energy to fight him as if that moment had, even before she first saw the man, burrowed itself inside her.

He shifted his eyes to Dalila's chest, and that is when she realized it was bare, her breasts exposed mercilessly to the stranger's brutal desire. In her heart, a ferocious thrumming. Shame and despair. She turned her head and clenched her teeth. Now she could deduce how she had ended up there. He had carried her and undressed her from the waist up, leaving her to her own devices. He had managed to bring her here through some clever means, perhaps some substance that had rendered her unconscious.

The man's rough hands touched her waist then slid up to her breasts. She meant to pray and even muttered the first words to *Hail Mary* but eventually resigned herself to a feeling of final, lost cause. She kept her eyes closed tight while he sniffled on her neck and rammed his fingers on her tender skin, and in a muffled voice, almost a grunt, whispered repeatedly a word she couldn't make out, as if it weren't directed to her. He was talking to himself, his mouth hard with tobacco razing Dalila's tremulous lips, licking her with a frantic tongue. She tried to repel him weakly while he carried on, his rabid saliva smearing her face.

She woke up and realized, between terrified and relieved, that her pajama top was missing. She found it, still damp with sweat and tears, by the foot of the bed. She turned on the light in an attempt to chase away the too-solid impression of the man from her dream, but he wouldn't let go of her, even as she was wide awake, in the safety of her home, her parents sleeping in the bedroom next door. And the rest of the night stretched into watchful hours for Dalila.

If only she had awakened before his apparition—and it wasn't her fault that he had inserted himself so violently in her dream—she wouldn't have the details of that face imprinted, and so very precisely, into her memory. The small eyes, the puffy eyelids, the round nose, the thin lips, the irregular, yellow teeth, the arrogant, perverse contours of his face. She would also be free from that stranger's smell and sour breath if she were master of her own dreams. How to lose the feeling of that body pressed against hers, the roughness of his hands on her breasts, the texture of his tongue and the bad taste of his mouth?

She bathed repeatedly, refilling the bathtub again and again, and spat dozens of times until morning, when it was time to go downstairs for breakfast, with the nocturnal, damned impression of that man's presence still on her. At school, she tried to pay attention in class, but the wretched smell still hovered around her, saturating the air she breathed. In her classmates, she saw the savage gaze that had only existed in her night. In her teachers' lessons, she heard the demented, repeated word in its undecipherable obscenity.

At night, her fear and suspicion were such that they occupied the entire space of her bed and displaced the fatigue that had consumed her all day. She wanted to forget about the man and the strangeness of that dream, but she had nothing to lean on to make sure that while she slept, he wouldn't come back to torment her. That was worse than anything she had experienced in all her fourteen years. And even if she could get over her embarrassment and went to find her mooring in her parents' bed and nestled between them, she still wouldn't be safe because she knew sleep was no man's land. Her own sleep, like a trap, could bring the dream and the man back.

Shortly before the new day dawned, she fell asleep unaware she was failing in her vigil, her eyes finally closing without her consent. But as that morning started, Dalila's dreams didn't bring her the man from the other night. Neither did they the following nights.

She settled back into a routine and while subdued when thoughts of the man crossed her mind, she didn't recognize right away it was him outside when she leaned on the windowsill to watch the movement of the street. There he was, in her own garden, crouched by one of the flower beds, a cigarette hanging from the corner of his mouth, his caved-in chest bare, his filthy hands rooting in the dirt she walked on every day.

She tried to step backward, and just like in the dream, her feet had turned into two chunks of lead. She didn't want to see him, and yet, there he was, so very close, deserter of her dream and usurper of her space and reality, lifting up to her his dreadful face, dragging her to him with the same quicksand eyes.

She still had time to scream. The garden, the flower bed, and the man blurred all the way to darkness. When she came to, lying in bed with her mother sitting by her side and holding her hand, Dalila wanted to believe it had all been but a feverish dream. She asked about the man in the garden, and her mother confirmed he existed. He was a gardener working for one of the neighbors, he came recommended, what had he done to frighten her that way?

Her words coming out in a jumble through her crying, Dalila told her mother about the nightmare from months before, the man who had molested her, and how she had been tormented by him the days that followed. Her mother tried to cheer her up, convinced that the man she had talked to that morning about taking care of her garden couldn't be the same one who had frightened Dalila in her dream.

Still hopeful she might have been mistaken, with her mother's help she walked to the window and saw him again. There was no question. He was the one who had cornered her in the darkness of that night and held her hostage in a bell jar of fear. How could she forget those hands that had defiled her body? How could she not recognize the degrading gaze that had taken away her peace so many days and nights?

Dalila begged her mother to send him away. Touched by the girl's anguish, she agreed and for the first time was worried about her mental health. Protected by the curtains, Dalila watched as the man was told to leave. She saw him get up, filthy with sweat and fertilizer, stick some bills in his pocket, grab a bag from a corner, pick up a lily from one of the flower beds, and walk out into the street without looking back. Or up.

When she had forgotten about him again, she ran into the man from her dream one last time. She was walking back from school with some friends late in the afternoon when a sudden, heavy shower forced them to disband. Those who lived far ran to a bus stop. The others made a dash to their homes in the pouring rain. Dalila stopped by a newsstand, where she bought comics and chocolate and waited for the downpour to let up.

On her way down the hill, an abandoned lot, evening falling. There he was. She halted in terror, a scream stuck in her throat. The man came towards her, dragging his leg. They faced each other, Dalila disarmed and motionless. Sinking into her hair, his hands stank of rotten plants.

She strained to turn her head so she wouldn't see him anymore and felt the cold ground crack open under her feet.

The next morning, Dalila's body was found nude and covered in bruises, a pink foam still seeping from her mouth. From her sex, a withered lily stuck out, speckled with blood.

Thy Neighbor's Wife

I ARRIVED first at the park where Ana Laura used to walk around by herself and sat at a bench a bit far from the path. I felt anxious and apprehensive. Were those rain-bearing clouds and that oppressive heat a bad omen from nature? Although I didn't want to guess the reason why she wanted to see me, I had been torturing myself since her phone call, wondering what she might have to say.

I saw her walking down the boulevard towards me, her steps heavy as if she were ill. Her long, firm legs no longer glided with elegance. She made her way over and sat on the bench without looking at me. I waited. I could barely breathe, and yet, I kept quiet, like a fearful, obedient child whose mother is upset. Many times I had left the office in the middle of the afternoon to see Ana Laura, but always and only to love her. Those had been, as far back as I could remember, the best afternoons of my life.

Now there we were, side by side, in threatening, almost unbearable silence. She looked intently at her shoes, leaning forward, shut off within herself, as if everything around her had disappeared. Ana Laura and her impenetrable inner world. A vast and free territory where she wandered, oblivious perhaps of me and my love for her.

The discomfort I felt before she arrived intensified as she turned inward. I feared if I asked her what had brought us there, I would hear the worst. And the worst, I knew, would be losing her. I was hesitant to even come closer, put my arm around her waist, hug her or stroke the back of her neck, as I always did when we got to be alone together.

For a moment I thought she was hiding her face in her hands because she was crying, and that unnerved me even further. But then she turned towards me, and I saw her cheeks were dry. She seemed like a different person, although those were the same eyes that had made such an impression on me when we met—long-lashed black eyes that pierced through things and people as if seeing everything for the first and only time. Eyes like tentacles that grabbed their prey and paralyzed it, eyes that seemed detached from Ana Laura.

"I want you to leave," she said suddenly in a firm voice. "Now. Leave us. Go somewhere far away. I don't want to see you ever again. My nerves are shot. I can't go on like this. I can't take it anymore. Enough!"

I didn't say a word. Not right away. A sense of annihilation spread all over my body. I didn't want to believe or comprehend it. I didn't want to accept what I had just heard. Ana Laura was kicking me out of her life. Just like that, with a dozen words, she was shattering my dream and bringing darkness into my day.

Perhaps it was fear interfering with my breathing. A block of ice had lodged itself in my chest, the neck muscles had contracted into a deep pain, and my hands grew damp with a cold sweat.

I held her head in my hands and turned it towards me. I pulled her close and gazed at her at length. She too suffered. A concentrated, dry pain was imprinted in her eyes. Stunned. A web of thin wrinkles like cracks on parched ground had made her skin saggy, her face shrunk, misshapen. For the first time, I saw her as an aging woman. As if in a foggy dream, the image I had in front of me grew distorted, an Ana Laura bereft of innocence, corrupted by the passage of time and pain.

"Why are you looking at me like that," she asked, looking away.

"No reason. I was just thinking I won't be able to live without you," I said, immediately embarrassed by a revelation that laid me bare and showed me weaker before her eyes than I already was.

"Don't be silly. Life is greater than all this, than the two of us, together or apart." Her petulant tone sounded fake to me.

"My God! What sarcasm!"

"It's not. You know it's not. I just want you to go away and put an end to this wretched story."

"Damn you! Why don't *you* go away," I said in defiance, looking her straight in the eyes to see what effect my words were having on her and suddenly finding myself taken over by violent feelings of rejection and rancor.

"I will, if that's what you want," she responded naturally, as if my question hadn't surprised her at all.

She wouldn't fight me. She had surrendered, as if any situation were more comfortable than the one which had kept us together. She despised me, for sure. She despised my lack of pride, my fragility, my pathetic insistence that I should have her forever. I grabbed her arm roughly. She groaned but didn't move. I had the urge to hurt her. I felt foolish, embittered and enraged, the protagonist of a ridiculous soap opera. So, that was it. Her intolerance of late, the headaches, the little digs. The evidence had been right in front of me, and I still didn't want to see that it was all headed to the end. I had felt it coming. But I couldn't admit it. Now it was happening and wounding me brutally. The worst part of it was not having any control over that pain, an almost physical pain, throbbing like an exposed nerve, like an animal skinned alive.

I was left with one choice: leave my own home or let Ana Laura go. I thought of my father right away. He would die if she disappeared. And I knew she might well do so. Once she told me that for some obscure reason, she always ended up harming those she loved. At the time, that confession disturbed me a bit, but I soon put it out of my mind. I had been so charmed by her that I would rather ignore anything that might cast a shadow over that feeling.

"Do you really want me to go away? Are you sure," I offered in a conciliatory tone. I wanted to show her I had calmed down and would be able to hear her without growing angry, although my blood pumped furiously in my veins.

She nodded.

It seemed suddenly astounding to me that one's life could depend entirely on someone else's decision. That a single word, yes or no, uttered with or without conviction, had the power to change the direction of so many things. It was terrible to realize that people had so much power over others that they could determine their destiny.

I had to think clearly, give some order to the chaos that had taken over my head. I was filled with resentment, guilt, and disgust for her and for myself. Before meeting Ana Laura, I had thought of myself as more ethical and generous than most people I knew. My father even told me, and more than once, that among his four children, I was the only one who had inherited his mother's essentially dignified nature, and this comforted me somehow, as I lacked the physical attributes enjoyed by my brothers, whom fate had favored. I hadn't been an attractive child. And as a man, I didn't draw much female attention. Sometimes, I would hear people say that absence of beauty was irrelevant when one had strength of character. Yet, I was convinced that because of my looks I had been somewhat neglected as a child by my family, especially by my mother, and became withdrawn and insecure as a teenager, used to being alone, to being an outsider.

Later, when I was about eighteen, the first woman with whom I lay was beautiful and experienced. After many nights together, she convinced me that I had strong arms and a masculine face and that I made love as if it were the last time and with the only woman on the face of the earth. I couldn't have been any better than I was. Since then, I stopped thinking of myself as a hopeless disgrace. I accepted myself as I was. But my sense of helplessness and self-pity never left me entirely.

It was Ana Laura, six years later, who really taught me about myself. With her, I perfected my lovemaking by becoming more ardent, more daring. I also turned out to be a cynical, cruel, shameless son, capable of the most despicable acts, the most perverse lies, paradoxically in the name of the most noble feeling of all—love.

There we were, Ana Laura and I, for what one might call the last adjustments. The end. In the silence that followed my question and her gesture of agreement, I recalled in a flash everything I had done those past few months to love her.

My brothers and I barely knew her when my father announced he was going to marry her, a woman twenty-two years his junior. We feared she might add frustration to the pain he had lived through, and we even tried to talk him out of it. Our mother had died two years before. Cancer had consumed rapidly and stupidly the woman he had shared his life with for forty years. The first fifteen months after that loss were a calvary to us. My father took to bed, and we resorted to all sorts of medical treatments to help him recover. And then, Ana Laura came along, and he told us he had been most fortunate. He had met her in the waiting room of a clinic, and since then dinners, weekend trips, and long phone conversations had pulled him out of a pointless routine of therapies and pills. We finally saw him happy and confident again, as he had been before our mother fell ill. It would be deplorable if the woman who had brought him back to life turned out to be a gold digger. We thought of our father as excessively vain and a bit childish, and we felt we had an obligation to protect him.

The first time we met Ana Laura, her politeness, kindness, and good nature proved disarming, and in short order she earned everyone's absolute trust. Almost everyone's because a secret, confused feeling prevented me from being at ease in her presence. I could sense in her something undefined, a question mark pricking my imagination. Beyond her benevolent and patient demeanor, which I could almost take for indifference, I divined the hidden existence of another woman, dense and dark like a new-moon night, an unsuspected Ana Laura of restless thoughts, visceral reactions, and complex emotions.

After that first encounter and up to the wedding five months later, I saw her every Sunday. She would come to have lunch with us and stay until evening. Sometimes, my brothers, their wives, and children would join us. Otherwise, my father, Ana Laura, and I would keep each other company and have a good time talking, cooking, or playing cards.

I would take advantage of those moments to find out a bit about her life. She lived alone in a little apartment crammed with books. She had never been married. An only child, her early years had been haunted by the loss of both parents in a car crash. Raised by a well-to-do and kind aunt, who had given her a fine education, Ana Laura made good use of what she had been offered. She had traveled a great deal before earning a degree in languages and literature. She made her living translating from French and English and teaching. At home, she spent her time listening to music, reading, or planning her lessons.

Whenever she left on those Sunday evenings, I would find myself slightly anxious, wondering what had led her there, to my father. Although Ana Laura was no longer young, she had a strange, captivating beauty. She had a keen perception of things and the gift of listening, which was rare among the people I knew. And besides all that, her gaze was most singular, unlike anybody else's. Undoubtedly, she had had many opportunities to get married. Why hadn't she? Why had she chosen my father, of all people? Was it the books that had brought them together? Both had a love of literature. Many times, in ignorant and dazzled silence, I witnessed their discussions about characters' lives and behavior as if they were real people, as if at any moment they could jump out of the yellowed pages and join like guests of honor our world of beauties and miseries.

At some point, everything I saw, heard, and touched began to transform, filled with the new and bountiful image of Ana Laura. And everything became clearer. And the people in my life or even the people on the streets seemed friendly, supportive, in kinship with me through that then-luminous feeling.

I started to wonder if I might be in love with my father's future wife. Overwhelmed by a blend of pleasure and fear, fascination and repulsion, I tried to downplay the conflict by telling myself Ana Laura was worthy of any man's desire. That's when I started to search for indications in my brothers that they too wanted her. I would watch their eyes, their gestures, their words. In the end, I envied them for being safe from her. I would tell myself absolutely nothing had happened between us anyway. Perhaps she didn't even think much of me. Perhaps she considered me too young, foolish, and inexperienced and only put up with me because I was the son of the man she loved. However, before they got married, I became certain the opposite was true.

Every Sunday, Ana Laura would arrive at around nine in the morning. She, my father, and I would sit on the porch in the sun, reading newspapers and chatting. Sometimes we would go to the market for fresh fish and seafood. Later, she would go to the kitchen, and the two of us would watch a soccer game or some show on TV. After lunch, my father would go lie down for a few minutes, as he did every day, and we would remain at the table. To hide my extreme disquiet, I would ramble on and on about the most mundane details of my days at the office, the cases I was working on, the family dramas, the crimes, the juries. What else could I talk to her about? She would listen to me, her chin in one hand, a demure smile on her lips. That was enough to warm my heart.

In those moments, I would search in Ana Laura some indication that would assure me I wasn't alone in that fantasy. A suggestive word or a more inviting gesture. Since I found nothing, I would convince myself momentarily, with relief but also frustration, that soon I would be able to free myself from that fascination. A strange fascination because she was not at all the type of woman I usually felt attracted to. Tall and thin, no curves, and white, very white. Besides—and this fact alone should compel me to snuff out this insane feeling that had taken me over—Ana Laura soon would be married to my father.

It happened on one of those Sundays, a few days before the wedding. She asked me to help her in the kitchen. My father had gone into the garage to grab his glasses, which he had left in the car. We were standing very close to each other, so close I could feel her breath on my face. Then our hands touched, and Ana Laura trembled and took a step back. We stared at each other for a few seconds, and that is when I could see clearly the look of desire on her face, her flushed cheeks, her parted lips, her flared nostrils, her fiery eyes boring through me, searing my body, clamoring for my love. When we heard the door slam, we remembered who we were and stepped away from each other.

That moment confirmed what I had doubted until then. That she was not indifferent to me. That Ana Laura wanted me. That Sunday, I couldn't bring myself to stay with them. I made an excuse and left, walking aimlessly, recalling what had happened, mad with happiness and horror. What had happened anyway? Everything. And so little. Enough to make me dizzy. There must have been a grain of madness in me, something to make me hurtle myself into space that way, knowing there was no net below to catch me. I felt big and strong. Euphoric.

I have asked myself many times why we feel attracted to some people and not others. What force pushes us toward someone we know or suspect to be inadequate, incapable of making us happy? Why can't we back out in the beginning, before circumstances pull us closer together? Why do we insist on risking everything by betting all our chips on the one person who doesn't deserve a single one?

I should have kept my distance but didn't. I chose to be near her, spinning around her light, like a suicidal moth. And I had to admit she had done nothing intentionally to seduce me. Who had seduced whom anyway? I didn't know. In fact, I had never been good at the art of seduction. I didn't even know how to behave around women. As a teenager, I envied my friends who seemed very comfortable approaching girls at school or on the street after a few exchanged glances and then starting to date them and show them off at parties, looking smug in their victory. I wouldn't even venture. I wasn't bold enough to flirt or try the pick-up lines and clichés that had the power to hit the girls' soft spot. I failed in my first two or three attempts. From then on, it was the girls, and only a few, who would come after me. And even if I were convinced one of them was interested, I would get all flustered in their presence and start doubting the girl and myself, which only exacerbated my sense of abandonment and isolation.

My personal hell started in the days following that Sunday. I tried desperately to read some message encoded in Ana Laura's eyes. There was none. No understanding. Or desire or embarrassment. She remained inscrutable. But she seemed too enthusiastic about her wedding preparations, as if what had happened between us hadn't affected her in the least. Or perhaps under that seeming invulnerability she was simply trying to protect herself, pretending what had happened didn't matter at all.

To this day I don't know why I allowed them to get married. I could have stopped them. I should have convinced her to stay away from my father. However, we had not been alone together since that Sunday. Besides, I feared behaving inappropriately or prematurely and losing her forever. Although I didn't know exactly how much, I knew I desired her a great deal. But I couldn't be sure she felt the same about me. The moment we had and wouldn't have again until she came back from her honeymoon could have been a mistake for Ana Laura, without any of the meaning it had had for me. What was I holding on to, then? A brushing of hands and a locking of eyes. Intense, yes. But nothing more. Everything too ephemeral to sustain my memory and hope.

I fell ill a few days after Ana Laura and my father returned. A virus knocked me down and sent me to bed for a week with a high fever, chills, and body aches. Ana Laura took care of me with the dedication of a mother. She would bring me medicine, take my temperature, give me cold compresses when my fever spiked, feed me juices and special soups she had made herself, and tell me tenderly that soon I would be better. But I didn't want to get better. I wanted to be her eternal patient, yielding and resigned, willing to comply with all her prescriptions, as long as she stayed forever by my side.

My body had felt numb during my illness but started to respond strongly at the first signs of recovery. Sometimes, Ana Laura just had to touch her hand to my forehead or sit next to me on the bed for it to happen. Mortified, I would turn to lie on my stomach, hide my face on the pillow, and say I wanted to sleep. She pretended not to notice, but soon I would learn how much she appreciated it. And when I was almost fully recovered and ready to resume my daily routine of work and other engagements, we made love.

I was sleeping soundly when I was awakened by her caresses. For a while I kept my eyes closed, still on the threshold of reality. I didn't know how long I had been there or if we had done it before. But the fact is, soon our bodies were pressed together, and we were kissing with the sweet fierceness of those who burn with desire, my fantasy finally materializing and taking root.

After that, we made love numerous times, despite the limitations of place and time. She surprised me with her ability to detach from reality, to take leave from the rest of the world, to love me as if we were strangers, without shame or guilt, without words, except the dirty ones, some almost brutal, which, repeated in whispers, took on a special meaning, as if they had never been uttered in the entire world.

Loving her became my path home. Her body, my lost paradise, my treasure map, my promised land. Never before had I given myself so completely to anyone, nor had anyone taken me in so voraciously. Away from Ana Laura's warmth, I felt constantly, even in sleep, that the earth was splitting under my feet and an abysmal darkness was swallowing me. I never told her about these inner tempests. Deep inside, I feared she would feel pressured and leave me. And so I kept suffering in secret, while she seemed in full control of herself and the situation, as if driven solely by the impulsiveness of her senses, the strength of her desire, which flowed from the depths of her like a river in rainy season, plentiful and turbulent.

In the presence of others, as if in tacit agreement we would put on our masks and play masterfully our roles of stepson and stepmother, treating each other with the expected courtesy. Nothing gave us away. Yet, any impatient gesture from my father would cause me a sort of nausea, and that would keep me up all night. I didn't know how much longer I would be able to stand it, facing him day after day with his friendly smiles and warm hugs. His very presence was an accusation, a reminder that I was betraying him. I also missed the genuine, loving bond we once had and which I, and I alone, had tainted and destroyed, while he remained unaware of it all. I was certain I would never be able to forgive myself and come to terms with what I had done.

In my hopelessness, I started making plans. I would leave the country. Before my mother's illness, I had been interested in going abroad for graduate school. My father had even encouraged me to do so. Now was the moment. I had to get out of that situation. But how? Ana Laura would wrap her arms around me, and I would lose all desire to leave. Love, desire, obsession, whatever had enslaved me was keeping me in invisible shackles, vanquished. And so I kept groping for a solution. And lying, hiding, pretending. That was my life now. No one had made it up or read it in a book. Only I could change it, though I lacked the strength to do it. Or Ana Laura could, as I would learn that afternoon in the park, when I asked her the questions I had long kept inside:

"Why did you marry him?"

"Why, because I love him!"

"What about me?"

"I love you too."

In my astonishment, I wanted to ask her how many men she had slept with and if she loved them all. It would have been so easy to hurt her. But I refrained. In my right mind, when my jealousy bowed to reason, I would discard that possibility. It was even hard to believe she could make love to my father. I thought she had married an old man with no vigor, though I saw him that way only because he was my father. I didn't think he was virile enough to make love to her. Until the night I was startled by their moans. That was disorienting. While I wandered around the house, unable to sleep or do anything else, the tramp was lying with my father, only to lie with his son the next day, seeking pleasure with two men in the same house. Were we all innocent? Then what was stopping her from sleeping with other men?

Driven out of my senses by that discovery, I announced at breakfast one morning that I was going to be traveling for quite a while. But when Ana Laura called me that afternoon, I ran home, crazy with a renewed, morbid desire, ready to love her in all my wordless desperation.

I couldn't expect anything out of that cornered, forbidden love. They would always be there, husband and wife, accomplices forever, in the bedroom next to mine. This is what everyone expected, as did I. There was no fooling myself. I would never have her the way my father had her, entire nights lying side my side, their warm, rhythmic breathing on each other's back, each other's face. I would never have her in the middle of the night, nor would I watch her sleep. I would never wake up to her holding my hand and whispering *I am here*.

What could I tell her? Everything I had held inside for fear of losing her? No. We were exhausted. She was depleted. It seemed to me she couldn't get away from there soon enough, though we would be sitting at the dinner table later that day, facing each other, in my father's presence.

I also had to go back to the office. Later I would talk to my father about my decision to travel for a while. Wasn't that precisely what Ana Laura had demanded of me? That is how it would be. I could anticipate what awaited me. First, the long agony of separation, the shattering of my senses, the difficulty of finding my bearings without the guiding star of those eyes, the image of her naked body solidified in my memory. Then, the adjustment. Finally, the forgetting.

With effort, I got up and walked away, feeling she was following me with her eyes. At the end of the boulevard, I turned around and saw, to my surprise and frustration, that Ana Laura remained in the same position on the bench, her head down, her eyes fixed on her shoes.

Broken Crystal

IT WAS you, wasn't it, Belmira? I know you can't hear me, now that you've gone someplace far away and there's no use thinking you'll come back someday. I'm all alone, except for our secret, and I don't even know how long I'll be able to keep it, because the note, forgive me, Bel, I think I left the damn thing at Antonio's house, I don't know exactly where, but in that moment of panic, I ended up dropping the envelope in the middle of all that mess and only realized I'd left it behind when I was already out in the street.

Ah, Bel, if I were given the gift of turning back time, just a little while, just until yesterday, so things could happen a different way. . . I should've taken better care of you, I know, I know quite well what a mistake it was to let you leave last night, when you seemed so hurt. I should've told you lots of things, don't be silly, he doesn't deserve your suffering, you going so far away from the people who truly love you; stay, Bel, don't despair, this too shall pass, I promise it will. But

I couldn't say a thing, with all those emotions drowning my voice.

Today it's too late, and you're gone. I was left with that note, which I actually don't have anymore, and this longing and this pain and this fear, a fear that's bigger than the biggest of fears, how can I explain? The terror of a nightmare. Why are we all so alone in nightmares, Bel? Only, now there's no way I can get rid of this one, and I won't ever wake up, because I'm not sleeping and everything I saw is real, just as I am real, as are the people who walk by me, the ground I walk on, the rain that falls, and the home I'm going back to, this time without you.

I should've at least walked with you to the bus station and waited for you to get on the bus. Isn't that what people do when they love each other and have to part ways? But it wasn't disregard, Bel, it's just that it was past eight o'clock and Mom was home, waiting for me so we could talk about the usual topic, you know, my lousy grades in school. What would she do when she looked around the house for me and found you too had disappeared with all your belongings? I don't even want to think about the fit she would throw. There—I think it was all her fault, you know? Because if I'd gone with you, nothing would've happened. I keep wondering what could possibly have been going on inside you last night to make you go a different way. I wanted to know when exactly you changed your mind and instead of going straight to the bus station you decided to go see Antonio for the last time. You weren't even angry when we said goodbye, no; just sad, very sad. I'm sure he was the one who infuriated you, and hurt you, and humiliated you, as he'd been doing lately, and you ended up having a really bad fight, didn't you?

Why didn't you tell me, huh, Bel? You could've called and told me, like this: *Ursinha, I'm so sorry, but something very bad happened and the note doesn't make sense anymore, tear it, forget about it, forget everything, and don't say a word to anyone.* Forget it, really forget it, I couldn't, but to betray your trust, never! Don't you know you're my best friend, Belmira? Not my best friend; my only friend. If you'd told me everything, you would've spared me a great agony, greater even than the pain of losing you. You knew full well how terrified I am of blood. . . Remember that time I fainted when the neighbor's dog bit off a piece of the mailman's arm? Oh, Bel, Belzinha, *why*?

I've been walking in the rain since I left Antonio's house. Even the sky seems to be crying for you and for him. If only the water that's soaking my clothes could wash away what's going on inside me. . . You leaving, the note, the blood, everything I saw would go down the gutters into the darkness of the earth and I'd go back to being clean, without memories, saved, Bel, saved! But the rain only makes me feel more abandoned, and I get the feeling that all those who pass me by know about me, about us. If feels like I'm walking around naked. With each pair of eyes, a pang of discomfort, of agony.

You know what, Bel? Fear, that darned fear, dark and sticky like a worm's belly, has wrapped around my legs and is making me stumble around. I don't know if I'll even be able to get back home. A woman has caught up with me and is looking at me weird; now she's offering me her umbrella. A knife-sharpener, who's found shelter for his grinding-wheel cart under an overhang, waves to someone across the street, a silver blade quavering in his hand. In my chest, drums rumble furiously.

If I'd taken a bus, as you might have advised me to, I would've escaped the water but not this misery. Every time I feel my mouth dry up and my stomach tighten, like now, someone always shows up to ask me: *are you feeling ill, Úrsula?* I can't crumble, Bel, not now, when I'm about to step into my home. A little longer now, just a little. When I get there, I'll run to my room, to my bed, and I'll hide under the covers. Mom can't see me like this, and if she looks into my eyes, I'm dead meat, she'll see right away the horror I carry with me and then, God forbid, I may, and forgive me for it, Belzinha, I may spill it all.

I know if you were in my place and I had written the note, you'd go back there to get it. I'm sorry, Bel, but I don't have the guts. It's all so monstrous! I think they'll find it, and it'll all be my fault. Why did I have to leave it there if Antonio couldn't read it anymore?

Shucks. I think I'm going to throw up. What I swallowed at breakfast, because Mom made me, is churning inside and making me gag, pushing from my stomach up to my throat and back. If you were here now, you'd have me suck on ice until I felt better, with that knack you have for convincing me of what's best for me, right, Belzinha?

A few more blocks and I'll be home. From my bedroom-refuge, I'll hear Mom's complaints, that you left us without so much as a goodbye, that ungrateful Belmira, after so many years and the kindness we've shown her, all we deserved was disregard. That was what we got for being so generous to the help.

I'll listen to it all in silence, isn't that what we agreed? We'd made so many plans. . . Too bad they didn't go the way you'd imagined. I did everything you asked me, Bel, but Antonio didn't come to the door, which was not closed, just ajar, and I couldn't even check whether he was as handsome as you'd said. I knocked twice, three times. Nothing. Is someone there? I pushed the door slowly and peeked inside, a bad feeling hammering inside, don't go in, Úrsula, don't go in, but I kept going, and then I found myself in the middle of the room, the note crumpled in my sweaty hand, my heart pounding. At that moment, I trembled, thinking of how Mom and Dad would react if they had any idea what I was doing. You know the feeling of a forbidden thing? Of a great sin staining your heart? So, I thought of you, Bel, the hopeless look on your face, your eyes red from so many tears, though the note said you weren't going to "cry over that goodbye," like the line in the Evaldo Braga song you liked so much.

Inside I found the windows closed and the lights off. I assumed Antonio was asleep. You'd told me that when he didn't have a job, he'd stay up late, and then he'd sleep in the next morning. I didn't know what to do, standing in the middle of a dark and strange room, with no one's invitation to remain there, but I couldn't leave without seeing him, because I'd given you my word, Bel, that the note, at whatever cost, would be delivered to Antonio, and besides, what I really wanted to do was look him in the eye, shake his hand, so he wouldn't question the trust you'd put in me, I knew everything, everything!

I walked across the room and almost tripped and fell over a bunch of bottles and empty glasses strewn on the floor. I pricked up my ears, where was he hiding? At any moment he could pop in through the door, see the intruder and get all upset, call me a nosy girl, and kick me out of his home, it'd be his right to do so, wouldn't it?

I opened a window and spent quite a while watching the disorder of all those things, albums, clothes, old newspapers, everything piled up on the couch. Cigarette butts, ashes, and plate scraps everywhere, and on the wall, a framed portrait of the girl that wasn't you. Ah, there she was. . . smiling at her beloved triumphantly, not prettier than you, my Bel, believe me! The moment I saw you, when you came to live with us, I thought to myself, that's the most beautiful girl I've ever met. But look, Bel, I'm not talking about that plasticized beauty of movie stars, who go to sleep and wake up without puffy eyes or messed-up hair. To me, the day you looked the most beautiful was when you dressed up as a flapper, remember? It was that *carnaval*, when you met Antonio. You looked like an angel. What do you think, Bel? An angel in a short, fringed dress, with long painted nails, mouth red with lipstick, a long cigarette holder, and a little pouch for confetti and streamers? Once you even confessed that had possibly been the happiest day of your life. And now I wonder why life does this to people, so much happiness and hope only to end up in such senselessness, which is you without Antonio and me without you.

And so, right there in front of me, in Antonio's living room, was a picture of the chosen one. Because of her, he'd left you. I looked away, sorrow pummeling my chest. Never, Belmira, will I be able to forget the night when he kicked you out of there and you woke me up to tell me, I'll never forget how you plunged your fingers into your hair and pulled it, and how you bit your finger nails and laughed and cried as you told me, he's going to marry someone else, Ursinha, the jerk, her portrait's there, I've seen it with these very eyes, it's hanging there on the living room wall for all to see, a girl from a nice family, just a little older than you, can you believe it? She's finished school, she knows things. He got tired of the maid, that wretch!

Oh, Bel, so much suffering! And you, of all people. A girl who's all kindness. So much loveliness only to end the way it did. I remember the day I asked you if love ever died, and you laughed as you answered, certain that yours was everlasting, when crystal breaks, it's because it wasn't real crystal. When I think of the things you told me about the nights you spent together, the kisses, the promises, the plans for the future, and the love! Ah, Bel, the love! You would tell me: when we make love, Ursinha, I think I'm going to die. And you didn't have to explain anything, because the words *make love* would echo in my ears, linger for hours in my imagination, stoke a fire in my blood. And so, Bel, when I think of all this, of what you had and lost, then I understand how love can turn into a dark night, into a ferocious beast, tormenting and devouring people, as it did to you.

Do you know when I knew for sure you'd been there? When I saw on the record player the Evaldo Braga album you were holding when you said goodbye to me last night. I saw the dedication on the cover poking out from behind the speaker, the same dedication seen so many times before, *To my darling Pomegranate, from your beloved, always, Antonio*. Why Pomegranate, huh, Bel? You never answered that question, and I'd still like to know.

I thought at that moment, can you imagine, that the two of you might've made up and fallen asleep together. That's when I decided to take a peek in the bedroom. The door was ajar. In the dark, it took me a while to spot Antonio, lying on the floor by the bed, shirtless, his arms straight down the sides of his body, as if he were asleep. On his chest, the medallion of Our Lady of Perpetual Succor that you yourself had bought to protect his body, protect him from all evil. I smelled something funny and thought it was booze. Maybe he'd gotten drunk because you'd left and had rolled out of bed after listening to the same song over and over, *I won't cry over your goodbye. . .*

I got down on my knees and crawled toward him. Then, I saw, Bel, the knife stuck in Antonio's neck and the pool of blood around his body, so dark and curdled it looked like chocolate syrup. I hid my face in my hands, but he remained there, so close that if he'd been alive, he could've touched my shoulder and pulled me in for a hug. I tried to move, but all I could do was moan, paralyzed as I was with fear, and what if I faltered and ended up falling on top of him, of all that blood? I don't know how I was able to breathe, Bel, I'd never seen a corpse up close, let alone a corpse like that, in such a pitiful state of abandonment, poor guy, without a coffin, a candle, someone to cry or pray for him.

How I managed to get out of there, I can't say; all I know is that I started backing up with my eyes closed, I didn't want to see him again, ever again, and I ended up bumping into a wall, frozen in terror, Holy Mary, Mother of God, help me, I repeated softly, very softly, as if my prayer might awaken Antonio, or rather resurrect him. My heart ached as if bathed in a blood stream of ground crystal, and my legs shook so much I don't know how I was able to walk out of the bedroom and then out of the house on my own.

Now, I'm walking into my home and you're not here to hold my hand and tell me you didn't do that, you didn't kill him, because that's what I'd like to believe, Bel. If you were capable of it, then I need to start unlearning everything you taught me about love between people and think from now on that love is not that beautiful or that generous, that love is hatred too and that when one turns into night, the other takes over everything.

Not Even the Stars
Are Forever

EVERY DAY has been sad since Mom got sick and Aunt Corina came to take care of us and our home. It has been a while. That was before summer vacation, and I am back to school already.

At first, I thought it was sheer boredom, that she was tired of me and my father and the life she was leading, and that was why she had given up trying to please him every which way and scolding me and punishing me so often. Even though she didn't seem that angry, these things must have set her nerves on edge. Besides caring for the two of us, she still had to keep up with her work at the newspaper and the housework. She always had to do more than my father and me; terrible things like washing, ironing, dusting the furniture, cooking, and still put up with his demands, and they weren't few. I don't think we were ever fair to her. Sometimes we would try to help, but he would get into a bad mood, and I would bungle it up so badly Mom would finally relieve us of the chores.

I was the first to notice she had been looking unwell. I felt a bit guilty, so from then on I tried to cheer her up every way I could, doing the right things, the way she likes, brushing my teeth after meals, taking two showers a day, studying for my classes, putting the dirty clothes in the bathroom hamper and the clean clothes in the wardrobe. I also started to spend more time with her, but Mom ended up resenting that new attention from me and telling me to forget about her.

I don't think my father even noticed her lack of interest in us and in everyday things, because he kept on going to work and coming home late, playing soccer on Friday afternoons, drinking beer with his friends on Saturdays, reading newspapers and napping on Sundays, while she was spending more and more time at home, almost always in bed, curled up under the sheets, doing nothing—my mother, who couldn't stand being still, who was always tidying up or cooking something. I meant to ask my father if he hadn't noticed the change, but I was afraid he would stare at me with those eyes of stone and tell me to go away, as he usually does when I am around.

I have always wondered why Mom likes him so much. Of course, there must be a reason, otherwise she wouldn't save the best part of the stew for him, ask me to be quiet when he is asleep, lower her eyes or soften her voice when he is irritable. Let alone allow him to hit me for no reason. I think she is afraid, like I am. I don't know for sure because she is not a child. She is pretty, kind, knows everything I ask about and more, other people treat her with the utmost respect. Why, then? Why does she put up with his threats that he will kick us both, mother and son, out of the house, the house where she has lived since she was a child, which she inherited from my grandparents?

In the past, when she was well, we would spend a lot of time together, without the snoop hanging around. Mom would call me *my angel*, and we would talk about unimportant things that made us laugh to our hearts' content. After she had checked my homework and finished all the housework, we would do crosswords and play Pictionary and even Name that Tune. Whether or not I won the game, she would hug me and sit me on her lap and kiss me and tousle my hair and delight me with a thousand tickles.

She also liked to tell me fantastical stories, and the best part is that they would never end. Just like in *A Thousand and One Nights*, she would always say she would finish them another day, and on that other day she would put off the end again. Princes, witches, ghosts, pirates, cave worlds, forests, ferocious beasts, precious stones, wars. She would tell me the best stories were inside us, in each person's imagination, and we just had to know how to tell them or listen to them to live better lives.

Now, that is all in the distance. Aunt Corina is attentive to me, to my father, and especially to Mom. I know she is doing us a big favor, because she has put her own life on hold, left everything behind to be with us. But she doesn't know how to tell stories or dream with me. She can't comfort me. She is not Mom.

When I am in bed, trying to sleep, I keep thinking of all these things, Mom's illness, the sadness that is her life now, the pain that makes her moan for hours and hours. My father is gloomier than ever and complains about everything. He started to sleep on the sofa-bed in the little TV room so that Aunt Corina can tend to Mom in the middle of the night without waking him up. Aunt Corina is patient and kind. She tells me he is suffering and deserves our support. I think she's right. He used to shave every morning and was always well groomed. Now, he doesn't care for those things anymore. Doesn't care about practically anything. And I feel relieved to be free of his harassment because he has forgotten about me. It even seems as if, with Mom's illness, I have ceased to exist. We barely see each other, and he doesn't even ask about me.

I don't know if it's possible for a father not to like his son at all. Once, when my classmates and I were in catechism, I asked the instructor, and she said no. She said that the love parents have for their children is the greatest and most sacred, that children are a blessing from God in their parents' lives. If she could see how my father treats me, she would understand why his presence terrorizes me, and I don't think she'd be comfortable giving me that same answer anymore.

It has been that way since I was much smaller. There must be something terribly wrong with me. I am less than what he wished for, I have failed in something but still don't know what, but one day, I swear, I will find out. If it were possible, I think he would push me back into my mother's womb. It wouldn't be that bad. Inside her, I wouldn't get to know the size of her suffering, and I wouldn't be afraid. I would be sheltered. And if she died, I would go with her, willingly, someplace where there was no father to interfere with our joy in being together.

Before Mom became bed-ridden, my father was always telling me to be quiet—why, if I always disappear into the shadows whenever he is home? He would also complain about my silence. He'd say he wondered from whom I had gotten my listless Punchinello ways, and that his only son was, to his great disappointment, an apathetic boy. I had heard that word so many times that one day I decided to look it up in the dictionary. Mom tried to cheer me up, saying that was silly, I shouldn't let it bother me, because, truthfully, he didn't think of me that way, it's just that he worked too much and was always getting upset with his boss or coworkers. This is another mystery. Why does Mom insist on protecting my father, on sparing him from all kinds of difficult situations? After all, he is a man, not a boy like me.

I seem to remember hiding behind her legs to escape my father's fury since I was very young. And when he drinks and his eyes grow harder and redder, I lock myself in my room because I know for sure he will come and pick on me. Sometimes, not even that gives me an escape. If I don't open the door, there's a good chance he'll kick it in. And at times like this there is no use in Mom trying to intervene in my favor. That makes it even worse because he starts to yell that she babies me, if she keeps it up she will spoil me, I will turn into a man-child, a faggot, and a faggot will have no place in his house, he will throw the wretch out in the streets, to go fend for himself, learn how to be a real man and respect mother and father.

I even thought once that, if I were sick like Mom, perhaps he wouldn't treat me with so much contempt. And if I died, who knows, he might miss me and even cry because I am only thirteen and his only child.

My father only realized there was something wrong with Mom the day she couldn't go to work because of the fainting spell. We were having breakfast, and she started to grow pale and say, *oh God, what is this? I feel awful. . .* She got up to go throw up in the bathroom, but she didn't make it. She collapsed midway, sprawled on the floor. My father carried her to bed and asked her if she got her period. She nodded and started to cry. I soon understood what he was asking. I think he really doesn't like kids. He called Aunt Corina to ask her if she could come and stay with Mom, then he went to work. Aunt Corina came, and that day I didn't even go to school.

The next morning, Mom got up feeling better, went to work at the newspaper, and the fainting episode was forgotten. By my father and Aunt Corina, and perhaps by Mom herself, but not by me. Adults forget everything, and so quickly. Maybe I'm wrong. Maybe they don't forget and only pretend to. Because what I see, hear, and feel grows in my heart day after day, and at night, when I lie down to sleep, I like to try and figure out what the others don't even remember anymore, or prefer not to remember.

I have said all my days have been sad since Mom got sick. But today may have been the saddest day of my life because I don't recall a worse day. I'd been lying awake for a while and got up for a drink of water. Before I made it to the kitchen, my father's voice startled me and stopped me in my tracks. I couldn't remember hearing him speak that way, ever, not to me, not to Mom, not to anyone. He sounded as if he were trying to convince a child of something, the way parents talk to their children when they like them. I tried to understand what he was saying, but he was speaking almost in a whisper. I wasn't dreaming. If he wished, my father could be mellow and loving, the way Mom was with me. But with whom? And why?

I was so afraid he would notice I was there I held my breath as I stepped closer. Through the gap between the wall and the door, where I was hiding, I could see the two of them. Aunt Corina and my father. She was sighing and sniffling a lot. I think she was crying. I'm not sure because from where I stood I could not see her eyes. My father was trying to hug her, but she was pushing him away and shaking her head without saying a word. He said it wasn't his fault, that whether by the grace of God or a twist of fate, these things happened, that he couldn't live without her, without her love anymore, that what he was feeling was stronger than him, that Mom didn't need to know, that she would never know, that she, Aunt Corina, could trust him.

I went back to bed with my heart beating with such violence I was afraid they would hear it. But I was unable to lie down, cry, or do anything else. So I ran to Mom's room, and as I saw her there, helpless, so small under the covers, it was hard to hold back my tears. She kept her eyes shut, but I don't believe she was sleeping. I think she would rather stay that way than see us or hear us. She is suffering, but she doesn't want to talk about it. That's the way she is. I know because I am the same way. Even in this we are alike.

I wonder what Mom thinks about, alone and silent for so long. Every now and then, Aunt Corina starts a conversation, tells her of me, how obedient I've been, my latest school paper, which was praised by the teacher, the medal I won in the chess competition. She talks about my father, the good commission he earned from the sale of a few apartments, relays the news she has read in the papers, the love affairs on the soap operas, the recipe she has found for next Sunday's dessert. But nothing sparks Mom's interest. Even when she has the TV in front of her, I know she is not paying attention to the shows because her eyes glaze over. Maybe she is thinking of herself, her illness, or me and my father, our lives without her.

She only leaves her bed to go to the bathroom or to the hospital, and when she comes back home, she looks more damaged than before. After the surgery, she grew thinner and paler. It seems to me she has shrunk. She walks like she's carrying an enormous burden on her back, she has lost her hair and feels nauseated almost every day. She still smiles when she sees me, but her smile is so lifeless I feel like turning my back on her and running out of the room. I know she smiles for my sake, so I won't feel sad, but I don't get very close anymore, and this is so weird because, truthfully, I want nothing more than for her to squeeze me in her arms and chase away my fear. Would it do any good to tell her this? She would get worse if she knew. Maybe she doesn't have the strength to hug me anymore. Besides, I might even hurt her. When she calls for me, I let her stroke my face, but this only fills me with more pity, for her and for myself.

Aunt Corina says that Mom has surrendered to her illness, and she shouldn't act that way. She should do things that give her pleasure, like walk along the beach, care for the garden, sunbathe, see people, talk. My father agrees with Aunt Corina. They are right, but Mom won't listen to them.

The doctor has gone as far as to say Mom is behaving as if she didn't want to get better, as if she would rather die. And I think I know why. If she is sick or dead, no one will be able to torment her or hurt her anymore.

I had never stopped to think about that, about the threat of being without Mom, of her being taken away from me. Mothers should be forever. But not even the stars are forever. My fear grows day by day. It grows along with the bad thing that invaded and took over part of her body. I know this, though Aunt Corina says it's not so, the tumor has been destroyed, and she is going to be well.

I want to think that way too, that she is not going to die, because there's no consolation to me in this talk that after death many people, my Mom included, will go to heaven, a place meant for the pure of heart, where there is no suffering, but also from where no one is allowed to return, no one has written a letter, or called to say how much they miss you. A place that cannot be found on any map, far to get to, impossible to leave. The infinity of God. That's what I have learned. And how cruel it is! I want Mom near me. I don't want to forget her fairy gaze. I don't want to forget I am her son.

Sometimes I wake up frightened in the middle of the night and go to her room. While Aunt Corina sleeps, Mom might be dying without anyone to hold her hand. How weird death is. Suddenly, the heart stops and blood doesn't run through the body anymore. Then, you are no longer there. This gives me chills. Life would be much simpler if mothers were born mothers, if all parents were generous and kind, and their kids were children forever, if no one got old or sick or died. How come God, who knows everything and better than anyone else, didn't think of this?

I keep wondering what would happen if Mom could guess my father's feelings for Aunt Corina. Would she stay in bed, indifferent to that too? Perhaps she would die from the pain. I am not talking about the pain that has punished her for so many months. I am talking about something much worse: the pain of being deceived by the person one loves the most.

We think that everything in life is a choice. Once, during mass, the priest talked about free will, and back home Mom explained what that meant. But my impression is that we choose almost nothing. I, for one, didn't choose to have the father I have, and I didn't choose to lose Mom. She didn't choose to get sick, either. And Aunt Corina didn't choose to have my father fall in love with her.

He told Aunt Corina these things happen and no one could stop him from loving her. But I wish I didn't know, I swear I wish I didn't know that it would be possible for a man to want his own wife's sister so badly, while his wife languished in bed, like a butterfly interrupted in its flight by an evil hand. Why?

There are so many *whys*! I want to go on believing that when I grow up I will have all the answers I need, though

Mom, who is very wise, has told me this will not be possible, because as we keep growing and then get old, some answers will show themselves, but other questions, some greater and more difficult, will come along too.

This why, my father's secret love for Aunt Corina, is as big and dangerous as the why of Mom's illness. And it seems that when we don't have anyone to ask, to give us an answer, the why starts to swell and rot inside us, like spoiled food. And even if I had the courage to kill my father, and I could do away with him somehow if I wanted to, without the two of us having to face each other, I would only have to figure out where in this house Mom keeps the rat poison, even so, if I killed him, I would still have all the questions throbbing inside my chest, even so, I wouldn't be able to mend the butterfly's torn wings or make it fly again.

Açucena

SO MANY years have gone by, and I still haven't learned how to get over Açucena. In my dreams and in my waking hours, she is always present, exactly as she was when we were first together—free, beautiful, fully herself, flower of desire and hope, summer splendor on her skin, ocean scent in her hair, salt in her smile, and that look of first girlfriend, all of this and, above all, the way she held me tight in her arms still makes me want to cry.

At first, we were happy—almost happy. Actually, from the beginning it bothered me that Açucena didn't know, or even held any suspicion, of the secret sewers running through me, the dark labyrinth of my fantasies, my wolves and vultures, the obsessions that little by little destroyed our dream. Sometimes she would ask why I rarely talked about myself. And I would tell her there was nothing to talk about, that my life had always been so sterile that only she and everything that came from her would interest and enrich me, that my life had started with my love for her.

She wanted to know, she kept asking, and I tried to hide my discomfort, laughing and telling her of spontaneous generations. She would smile too and nod, as if it were possible to believe me. I didn't want to tell her about a father I knew nothing about, of a woman who had vanished without a trace, whom I could have called mother if I wanted to. Yes, I went to school, played ball, made a few friends, met women, but I never told Açucena about my difficulties with all this or about the millions of phantoms that had haunted me since childhood. I fear if she knew as much, she would love me less or even stop loving me.

I gave her a little or a lot, I don't know, of my own internal reservoir of light, if there was any left in the hell I had always endured. From morning when we awoke to night, we had so much—sea, streets, people, words, life brimming with sunshine and pleasure, and knowledge and consecration, everything so new and spontaneous it was hard to believe it was happening to me.

She came and gave of herself, eyes, lips, hands, skin, hair, fluids, as whole as her poetry, a miraculous tenderness. And for quite a while my demons withdrew, cornered by the magnitude of that devotion, exorcized by the goodness of that feeling.

Açucena loved me in her own way. At first, boundless, luminous. As the years went by, light-hearted and easygoing. Fervor and dedication, I know now, she only had for her poetry. Late into the night, struggling with the words, laboring over her verse, a treasure she would entrust to me the next morning. There they were, innocence and sin, sweetness and fierceness, abandon, madness, condemnation—poems that spoke of life and death but didn't reveal her. A word then, more than a word, I knew that well, was a shelter from pain. She had that. She was safe. I, on the other hand, only had my love for her, a whirlpool of hidden forces, missteps, temporary answers.

Jealousy. I don't know exactly when it took over me. I was jealous of something I couldn't define but was deeply ingrained in Açucena, a larger feeling, something I felt hopelessly excluded from. And it wasn't enough to hear her whisper *I love you so much* with a smile, her hands gently messing up my hair, her nose touching the tip of mine. She might as well have said, *I'm going to the movies with a friend* or *don't wait for me for dinner, I will be out late.*

One night, after we made love, I told her how much I missed the excesses of our first times together, the care she used to lavish on me, the fantasy of that love as my sole certainty, the embrace in the middle of the night and the confirmation that her body was there, tethered to mine, sufficient in its warmth and welcome. She heard me and kept quiet, her gaze fixed somewhere undefined. At that very moment, I divined something cruel and final was building up inside her.

There was no denying it. Every day, Açucena's eyes pronounced our union irreparably broken. I had the urge to beat her up until she bled, chew her up slowly, chain her to the foot of our bed until her poetry was composed once again only of her love for me.

What love? I was starting to question whether she had ever truly loved me. And yet, she herself had showed me love was like the moon, full, then waning, then crescent again, one side lit, one side dark, and even in sadness and boredom, it matures and reinvents itself, always translating its destiny of love.

I spent my nights watching her sleep, anxious with a desire that took my breath away and threw me into a death wish. Something sharp and dark scraped my chest inside, and I wanted to scream, but I didn't so I wouldn't wake her up. A cold, sticky sweat covered my body. I struggled to breathe. I feared I would die, and she would be free of me. Picturing her having sex with another man terrified me. And so I found myself worse off than I was before I met her. Weaker, pettier, crazier.

What to do if redemption came with the comfort of her arms, the sight of pleasure floating in her eyes? I started to doubt even that. The words and gestures that celebrated her love for me. Were hers the salt of her sweat, the madness of her tongue, the scent of the sea in her sex, the breath of her life? And as soon as her body detached from mine, I would again be consumed by suspicion.

Did her coming back home at the end of each day mean she still wanted me? I knew couples who stayed together for many reasons, noble or trivial, but not for love. What if there was someone else? Açucena's unfocused gaze, her feeble kiss, her body no longer hungry for mine, wasn't her whole body tattooed with that third presence between us?

Just as I tried to keep my ghosts from rising to the surface, so did she sink into the light-shadow of her poetry. She had become known and respected in the literary community. Many friends would show up at our home, and she would welcome them kindly while I hid in the bedroom, restless like a caged animal, a dart stuck in my chest. Occasionally she would be invited to artists' gatherings too. I accompanied her a few times, impressed by the ease with which she moved in a world that wasn't ours, where people behaved as if on a stage, performing lackluster roles ever more poorly.

Esteemed by many, for her person or for her poetry, Açucena seemed to enjoy our home and my company less and less. She was slipping, and I, terrified and now unashamed, would accuse her of inflicting those absences on me with the intent to crush me. She would shrug with indifference, still refusing my love.

At some point she started to lock herself in the bedroom on the pretext she was writing, and I would be left on my own, adrift, the night and I dragging along through the house bathed in the monotonous sound of the waves crashing on the shore and the strong smell of salt, as strong as my anger, frustration, and helplessness. My demons came back to life, and my world was again nourished by their voices. Whisky warmed me up, while the night wore away, and the morning mist would find me exhausted, sprawled on the sofa, on the rug, or by the door outside the room where she hid from me, like a dog forgotten by his owner and left outside.

I don't recall exactly when our bedroom hell-paradise started, but I know I was the one who dragged her into it. I and the load of insanity and fear I carried. I wanted to possess her beyond the tepid reality of her sex, beyond the essence of her poetry. What was Açucena thinking? That she could tease me and confuse me, sabotage what was best in me, my love for her, without consequence?

She didn't protest when I started to insult her and hit her during sex. Açucena seemed to enjoy what I thought would tear her down. I didn't recognize her. And I feared that game of dangerous words and physical abuse would end up casting us away into the ultimate abyss. Afterwards, I lacked the courage to tell her how astounded I was at that other woman, the intruder, the mare I would ride and ride furiously, clinging to its sweaty mane, hypnotized by those eyes clouded with desire and pain.

I wanted to set us free from those deep nights of despair, but that could mean I would be left with empty arms. What to do? I felt like an insect allured by light, one of those that get blinded and singed by the heat and yet keep on spinning around the lightbulb until they die, incapable of flying away.

Out of bed, our gazes would collide. And my jealousy grew to enormous proportions, out of control. To the suspicion of a lover, I added several. Açucena had turned into a lustful woman, and from her insides came the warm, thick odor of sperm and blood. I could sense the violence of her desire. So, one lover was not enough, nor was she satisfied by my imagination, or the imagination of my insatiable demons, which laughed and spat in my face, *look it, you wretch, look at the deplorable trail you leave wherever you go, look what you've done to the woman you love, you corrupted her with your madness and rottenness, you filled her with darkness and horror, and now, you bastard, you don't know what to do with it.*

I thought I would follow her, catch her in the company of some man, humiliate her, but I don't know if out of cowardice or, improbably, a bit of dignity left in me, I merely waited, an hourglass of agony, for the truth to emerge and free me, as if I truly believed such sad confirmation could possibly set me free.

Reduced to my powerlessness and holding onto an obsession that made me sick to my stomach and nourished me at
the same time, I started to gather, here and there, fragments
of conversations on the phone, ambiguous phrases, contra-
dictions, and even poems. Açucena wouldn't spare me, more
and more inaccessible, and as if to say, "here, take this pain, it
is yours, take care of it, cry over it on your own and leave me
alone." She was going, going, she had forgotten that her life
had become mine, that there was so much of her in me that
by destroying me, poor Açucena, she was destroying herself.

Whenever I was finally able to sleep, I would wake up feeling as if I had been thrust into a sort of vacuum and would
check that indeed there she was, she wasn't gone yet, she still
lay by my side, my anchor. I would whisper her name many
times and beg her, in a very small voice, like someone praying
late at night to flee the horror of a recent nightmare. I would
beg her not to leave, to allow me to be next to her, and in
return I would promise not to touch her until she was ready
again for my love. Açucena wouldn't hear me even when she
was awake. She wouldn't see me. I had turned into something
she knew was there, quotidian, at hand. Useful somehow.

That last night, I understood the pleasure torturers must
feel. I planned the boat ride in the open sea on a full moon
night. I chose the boat, the music, the wine. The sight of blood
dulls my senses, and I wanted to be fully alert to register
Açucena's every gesture, word, and expression in my memory.

That she agreed to come with me was the most surprising part. She was terrified of deep waters because she couldn't swim. We hadn't said a word to each other in days. Perhaps fate was really greater than life.

That is how I saw her lost to me forever, aware that without her, there would be nothing but my own helplessness. I will never forget the astonishment of my name in her mouth or the expression on her face in stark relief against the silver-black mass of water. Dozens of times, before her body was finally dragged down completely, she cried out to me, her lover and executioner, asking for clemency. I didn't cry. The pain was much, much deeper. I threw up when I set foot back on shore. The day was dawning, and my fear was gone. Açucena would now compose her verses in the silence of plankton, lichen, and mother-of-pearl.

Would there be an after? I did not care. I couldn't be worse or better than I was. Than I am. Innocent.

MARÍLIA ARNAUD is a critically acclaimed author from João Pessoa, Brazil who has published award-winning short story collections, a children's book, and three novels: *Suíte de Silêncios* (2012), *Liturgia do Fim* (2016), and *O Pássaro Secreto* (2021). *O Pássaro Secreto* was selected from 2,400 original works as the winner of the 2021 Kindle Prize in Literature in Brazil. Arnaud's short stories and novel excerpts appear, in Ilze Duarte's translation, in *Words Without Borders, Michigan Quarterly Review, Asymptote Journal, Exchanges Journal, Northwest Review, Columbia Journal Online*, and *Massachusetts Review.*

ILZE DUARTE is a recipient of the 2024 Sundial House Literary Translation Award. She translates works by contemporary Brazilian authors and writes short prose of her own. Her essays and short stories appear in *Hopscotch Translation, Thanatos Review, FlashFlood, Dear Damsel, Please See Me*, and *New Plains Review*. Her translations have been featured in *MAYDAY Magazine, Asymptote Journal, Exchanges Journal, Northwest Review, Columbia Journal Online, Massachusetts Review, Ambit*, and *Your Impossible Voice. The Book of Affects* is her first published book-length translation.